revive

marley valentine

Cover design by **PopKitty Designs**
Edited by Ellie McLove at **My Brother's Editor**
Book design by **Inkstain Design Studio**
Proofreading by **Hawkeyes Proofing**

revive

MORE BOOKS BY

MARLEY VALENTINE

Devastate

Deviate

Reclaim

Revive

Rectify

Devilry

Smuttily Ever After

Marley's Motherfuckers

I love you

x

prologue

HENDRIX

Looking outside the kitchen window, I see my family sitting around the outdoor table, laughing and eating. It's the happiest they've all been in a long time, and Jagger's finally where he's meant to be. His girl sitting on one side and his daughter on the other.

It's been hard for him, and he deserves every good thing in his life, but days like today feel like a punishment. A reminder of all I don't have and everything I want.

I lower my head in shame and let the familiar need of longing and jealousy consume me. This is why I need to get out of this place. Travel the world and put some space between my past and my present. I can't waste any more time, I need to hurry up and chase my fucking future. Whatever it is.

Unexpectedly, I feel a small hand putting pressure on the middle of my back. My body freezes, knowing there's only one other person missing from the picture-perfect family out in front of me.

"Drix." Her voice is low and needy, the familiar nickname sounding foreign on her tongue. "We need to talk."

My hands grip the caeser stone bench in frustration as I shake my head at her request, "I don't think there's anything left to say."

"Please." Stepping closer, the scent of her perfume seeps into my resolve.

I exhale loudly, knowing like always, the sight of her is going to have me questioning my decision to leave. She steps back as I turn to face her, and I'm already missing the simple touch of her hand.

I hate myself for it.

I hate that all roads lead to her.

Her short honey blonde hair falls in soft waves around her oval-shaped, porcelain face. Staring at me with such desolation and emptiness, and I hate that this look is only reserved for me. Her whiskey coloured eyes that lose their light when I'm around, bore into mine. Now that I see her, the way she stands, the way she's nervously chewing on her bottom lip, I know.

I know the girl I've loved for my whole life has come to break my heart one more time.

A constant push and pull, we've been at it for years. One step closer, three steps back, it's time to forget all we were, and all we could've been, or at least try.

I need to rid her from my mind, to find another focus. She's been my centre for too long, and I'm done spinning around her. It feels selfish and wrong to leave so soon after Jagger's release, but my options are limited.

I need to be immersed in a world where there is no risk of seeing her. Where the sun rises and sets at a different time, where I can finally breathe. Finally be me.

"Sasha, I can't do this right now."

"I need this, Drix. Before you go, I have to tell you how I feel. I have to apologise." The air crackles. "I have to say goodbye."

"Okay. Goodbye," I spit out, doing my best to appear emotionless and detached.

"It's going to be strange without you."

"It'll be better without me." She shakes her head in disagreement, and I welcome the challenge. "Ask me to stay."

"Drix," she pleads, averting her eyes. "Don't."

The words become too much, my heart cracking at the painful revelations. "I've got to go."

"Wait." Holding on to my hand, she pulls herself into me. Standing on the tips of her toes, she presses her body to mine, and kisses me. Quick.

Time stops. A single moment to process. A single moment to realise that's never going to be enough. Reaching out, I take hold of the back of her neck and pull her to me. Smashing my mouth to hers, I steal the kiss I believe I've earned.

I capture her moan, and I drown out the noise. Rough and

frantic, our teeth clash, our tongues duel, and the desperation between us becomes gut-wrenching.

The sound of the back door opening has me lifting her up, and wrapping her legs around my waist. In a few long strides, we're in my room, bodies pressed on to the back of the door, mouths melded, both of us refusing to come up for air.

My body's vibrating with hurt and anger, while my dick is throbbing with need. If this is it for us, we may as well burn in fucking flames.

Moving us to the edge of the bed, I lie her down, and she shifts. In one swift movement she takes off her dress, deep purple lace covering the parts of her I'm itching to see. Reading my mind, she takes off the last bits of her armour, and meets my eyes with unfiltered desire. Seductively she crawls to the centre of the bed, her ass up, back arched and flushed face ready and waiting. I can't get to her quick enough.

I shuck off my jeans and underwear, and pull my t-shirt over my head. Dropping each knee on the soft mattress, I kneel above her, naked and hungry.

Palming my cock, I focus on her pale flesh, dusty rose nipples, and round arse; my mouth and hands tingling in anticipation.

Unable to restrain myself, I lunge at her.

"Why?" I ask in between kisses. "Why do you want to give yourself to me now?"

Her eyes find mine, tears building up as they take me back to when things weren't complicated, when things weren't hard, and when she was unmistakably mine. "We need more good memories."

My hands find her tits, my tongue tracing her nipples; over and over, never getting my fill. She runs her hands through my hair, sinking her nails into my scalp at every wet swipe. My dick rubs against the bedding as I glide my mouth down her body, the friction providing the smallest relief.

I stop at the top of her slit, my breathing heavy, my heart racing. I close my eyes, trying to slow it all down. But she pushes her hips up, letting her needs be known. Her intoxicating scent makes it impossible for me to hold off any longer. My tongue parts her pussy, licking, and tasting. I tease her clit, flicking and biting.

"Drix," she cries, and I know the sound of her wanting to come is one I'll never forget. Wanting her to feel me on every part of her, all at the same time, I thrust two fingers inside her. "I'm so close," she groans. Rocking herself into my face while my dick begins to leak at the sight of her. My tongue laps at her clit, and my fingers twist and push farther inside of her.

Peering up at her, I memorise this very moment. Hooking my fingertips into just the right spot, I watch her stomach and legs begin to shudder. Head back, neck stretched, body arched, and her orgasm all over my face.

This is my paradise.

As she comes down from the high, she watches me, anticipating my next move. I rise and her eyes fall to my thick and needy cock.

"It's yours if you want it," I tease. Wordlessly, she sits on her knees, her mouth in direct line with my shaft. She circles her delicate fingers around me, and I hiss at the contact. Stroking up and down, I grow harder in her hands. She lowers her head, licking the tip before sliding me deep down her throat.

"More," I growl as I thrust ferociously. Selfishly, I fuck her face, and she takes all of me. I curse the gods above as I grab her head, and empty myself without warning into her mouth. Again, I memorise this very moment. How flushed her face is, and how tender her lips look; she's both alluring and submissive, swallowing every drop of my come.

This is my paradise.

Lifting her up, we both kneel, our eyes locked on one another. The salacious moments of earlier pale in comparison to what we know is coming next. I cup her cheeks, kiss her lips and let our bodies fall to the bed.

Her legs drop open slightly, and the silent invitation has me hard again in no time. Lining myself up, I push into her, and a noise akin to bliss leaves us both. Finding a rhythm, our bodies move with ease and familiarity.

Unable to look anywhere else, I stare into her amber eyes, as tears stream down her face. With every thrust, I give her all of Hendrix Michaels. My happiness and my heartache, both which have been at her mercy. And she's right, it needs to end.

"I'm sorry," she whimpers.

I catch her cry, apologising to her the only way I know how. She clings on to me for dear life, while we make love for the first time, and the last time. My body gives her the last fifteen years while my heart prepares to close it self back up for protection.

Together we pick up the pace, the love and hate between us pushing us farther off the cliff. Each stroke drags along the walls of her pussy, and I feel her start to quake.

Harder.

Deeper.

I bury myself in the only place that can hurt and heal me. Her nails dig into my shoulders and I pull back, thrusting with reckless abandon, watching her come undone one last time.

"Drix. Drix. Drix." My name falls out of her mouth like a prayer, each heady pant echoing around me.

"Come for me, Sasha," I order. "Let me remember you like this."

After fifteen long years, we both finally fall off the edge, our hearts shattering as we land.

This is my paradise.

one

HENDRIX
EIGHT MONTHS LATER

With my jacket thrown over my shoulder, I hold onto a suitcase with each hand, rolling them down the airport exit ramps. Leaving customs, there's a swarm of people on either side of me, desperate to get outside and meet up with their families. Sluggish from the fifteen-hour flight, my steps are slow, dreading the next hour it will take to get home.

It's been eight months since I left Sydney. Some days were long, but most weeks were fast. After I spent the first few weeks wallowing in the pain of my broken heart, I challenged the world to heal it for me. And as best as she could, that's what she did.

Looking out into the crowd, I search for a sign with my last name on it. I organised a shuttle bus to take me home. No hassle.

No fuss.

In the corner of my eye, waving arms catch my attention. Turning, I'm shocked to see Dakota, my fifteen-year-old niece bouncing around excitedly on the spot. I feel the smile spread across my face with ease at the unexpected relief of seeing a familiar face; more importantly hers.

Dakota is the most remarkable human being on the planet, and undeniably my favourite person. We have an unusual bond, forged through some strange circumstances, but the fact that she's here when I told her not to be, doesn't surprise me. Selfless in ways no other teenager is, I'm lucky to have her in my life.

Jagger, my brother, and Dakota's dad stands beside her, his arms wrapped around his girlfriend Emerson's waist, who is happily leaning into him. Wherever Jagger is, Emerson follows, and I wouldn't have it any other way.

After spending twelve years in prison, this is how his second chance should be.

Walking toward them, the crowd separates, Dakota running straight for me. I drop my backpack, and free my hands of my suitcases, catching her in a big bear hug.

"You're here," she squeals.

I chuckle at her excitement. "In the flesh."

"We're so happy you're home," she says as I put her feet back safely on the floor. At the mention of others being happy to see me, I look around, scanning our surroundings for brown eyes I know won't be here. Eyes I shouldn't be looking for.

Jagger waits for my gaze to land on him, giving me a sad smile and slight shake of the head. She didn't come.

Shaking hands, he pulls me into a one-armed hug. "Nice to have you back, bro."

"It's good to see you too." Letting go of one another, I lean over and give Emerson a hug; long enough to irritate Jagger.

"You guys didn't have to come and pick me up."

"Don't be silly," Emerson chides, while looking over at Dakota with a knowing smirk on her face. "It's not like we had a choice anyway."

Placing my hand on Dakota's head, I ruffle up her hair. "I missed you too, kid."

"Don't," she whines dramatically. "Do you know how long it takes to get my hair looking this good?"

Wrapping my arm around her neck, I pull her close so we're walking side by side. "Shouldn't you be at school today?"

"I took the morning off."

I gasp in mock horror. "But you hate taking days off school."

She laughs at my theatrics. "It's not a whole day. I just didn't want to miss you coming home." She looks down at her watch. "I'll be back after recess, and Mum agreed it would be a nice welcome."

The mention of Sasha brings the reality of coming home crashing down all around me. The young girl in my arms, with a smile a mile wide isn't someone I can avoid. She's my brother's daughter. My niece. My blood. But she's also a blatant reminder of someone I thought I had done well to forget.

This is why living overseas was perfect, I thought of her on my own terms. Usually when I was chasing the end of a bottle, or conjuring up images of her body while another woman was underneath me. Relentlessly trying, and failing to recreate the high from being inside her.

It's taken longer than it should've to finally realise Sasha will always be a scar on my heart. A deep cut held together by one single fraying thread; threatening to tear open and bleed over every bit of progress I make.

I don't want her to be a setback anymore, or a dull ache I need to learn how to live with. I don't want to think of her with hate, regret or bitterness. We both deserve better than that.

I just want her to be in the past.

A memory.

An experience.

A movie I once watched.

A song I once heard.

I want to remember her and I for exactly what it is... A moment that was.

"I'll be back after school." Dakota's voice brings me back to the present. "Dad's going to drop me off on our way home, and you're going to sleep while I'm gone."

"Oh, I am, am I?"

"Yes. Dad, tell him he needs to sleep." I turn to Jagger, and we both laugh at Dakota's bossy nature.

"I'm going to take him home after we drop you off at school. I'll even tuck him in and kiss him on the forehead."

She rolls her eyes. "Whatever. Just make sure you have all your photos ready, so I can see whether you listened to any photo taking tips I gave you."

"Yes, ma'am." I salute her. "I'll be ready and waiting."

I roll over in my bed, waking up to voices outside in the living room. The lack of light outside reveals I've been asleep for a lot longer than I intended. My muscles feel heavy, my mind fighting against my eyes wanting to stay awake. The time change, and the comfort of sleeping in my own bed is enough to feel like I've been anesthetized.

Throwing off the blankets, I swing my legs off to the side and lean my elbows on my thighs, my head in my hands. I need a shower.

A light knock sounds at the door, and the creak of it opening, has me watching to see who will come in.

"Hey man, did I wake you?" Jagger asks.

"Unless I sleep sitting up, no, you didn't." I rub my eyes with the heels of my hands, adjusting to the intrusion of light from the outside. "I was about to get up and have a shower, is everything okay?"

"Yeah, I'm just saving you from Dakota. She's about three

minutes off beating the door down, and turning the smoke alarm on to wake you up."

"Patience isn't her thing, huh?"

"Not today."

"I missed her too." I tilt my head toward the en-suite. "Give me ten, I'll be out soon."

"Drix," he stalls.

"Yeah?"

"Dakota's not the only one who missed you."

"Aw, tell Em I missed her too."

He shakes his head and smiles. "Fuck you."

Turning on all the lights, I head for the bathroom and let the steam from the hot water fill up the small space before standing under the heavy spray. I roll my neck and let the heat relieve the tension from my head, shoulders, and all the way down to my back. I get lost in the small luxury of having endless amounts of hot water at my disposal, sponging and scrubbing every inch of my skin, more than once.

Pressing the stainless steel handle down, the spray stops and I yank the hanging towel off the top of the glass door. Drying myself off, I step into the room and rummage through the small pile of clean clothes and find a random pair of lounge pants and a t-shirt and quickly throw them on.

"Surprise." Three familiar yet off key voices fill the room, followed by the bang of party poppers and multi-coloured streamers launched in my direction.

"What's this?" I ask, knowingly.

"It's your welcome home party." Dakota's innocent smile lights up every corner of the room. "We've got some food from every place you visited, and you can tell us a story and show us pictures when we stop at each country."

My eyes flicker between Jagger and Em who, like everyone else who meets her, are completely caught up in Dakota's enthusiasm. "Let's get this party started then shall we, I'm starving."

"Wow, these places are beautiful." Dakota taps her fingers on the keys of my laptop, flicking through all the photos I took while I was away. As breathtaking as the scenery was, there's something oddly satisfying in being here and hearing the sliver of envy in everyone's voices as I relay stories and show off souvenirs. It's a constant reminder of how I took the plunge and did something so out of character.

It feels years too late, but I try not to focus on that. My hands have been tied for so long, and I did what I had to with the cards I was dealt. There's no rush now, I just have to promise myself, at least for a while, I am a priority.

Wide eyed, Dakota stares up at the three of us, in some sort of trance. "I can't wait to go to all these places." Looking down at her hands, she counts silently with her fingers.

"What you doing, baby girl?" Jagger asks.

"I'll be finished school next year, and as soon as I turn eighteen," she points at the screen, the photo of Valletta, the capital city of Malta at sunset. "I'm going there."

A small crease forms in between Jagger's brows and Emerson instinctively rubs circles on his back in comfort.

"It's a little bit early to be planning, isn't it? What if you want to stay here? Or go to University first?"

"University," she blanches. "I'm not going to go to University. Not until I've taken photos of the world."

"You can't do that after?" No matter how much time has passed, I still know my brother like the back of my hand, and my heart breaks for the man who just got his daughter back only to lose her to the world and have no way to stop her.

"I can. I just don't want to."

Jagger would never push her, or tell her she can't go. Not when he holds so much guilt for the twelve years of her life he missed, but that doesn't mean when the time comes, he's going to give in so easily. The problem is, neither will she.

"I think you should just wait and see how the next two years plan out." Letting Jagger know I have his back, I try to steer the conversation away from the inevitable argument. "You might not even want to travel, by the time you finish school."

A loud knock dilutes the tension before it has a chance to erupt. I look at Jagger. "You expecting someone?"

"It's probably my mum," Dakota answers.

"I thought you were staying here tonight." Ignoring me,

Jagger heads to the door and Dakota grabs her bag from the kitchen bench and meets her parents.

"Are you ready? We need to go." Sasha's hurried voice travels through the house, and I bite the inside of my cheek at her irritated tone.

"Wait," I call out a little too loudly. In two large steps I'm standing beside Jagger and staring at the woman who looks different, but her presence still suffocates me the same as always. "Hi." My greeting is stilted and void of any affection, yet civil enough for our audience. "I have a gift for Dakota. Just let me get it from my suitcase."

Giving me a slight nod, she drops her chin to her chest, hiding her face from me. It stings.

She steps back into the darkness. "I'm going to wait in the car."

Speechless, I push back what just took place and retrieve Dakota's present. Wrapped up neatly in a map of Rome, I hand her a photo book I had made specifically for her. "Open it at home," I instruct. Filled with photos I purposefully kept hidden from her viewing tonight, I know these will seal the deal on her future plans, knowing I'll be the mediator between her and Jagger when the time comes.

With a look of understanding, she stands on her tiptoes and kisses me on the cheek. "Thank you. I'm glad you're home."

"Me too."

"I love you."

"Always, kid."

Leaving Jagger and Dakota to their own goodbyes, Emerson's eyes find mine, paired with an apologetic smile I don't understand. Choosing to ignore her, I begin to clear the dining table. Minutes of sharing the same space as Sasha and I can't ignore the fight or flight mode my body goes into. Eight months without saying a word to her, seeing her, or breathing the same air, and it all means nothing. I want to punch something. I want to scream and throw shit around like a mad man. I just want some fucking peace.

"Drix." Jagger's voice cuts through my internal rage. "Can we talk?"

Eyes watch me with caution and I feel even more out of place; unease taking over the usual sense of security I've felt in my own place, around my own family. "What's wrong?"

"Nothing, just grab a beer and sit back down. We want to tell you something."

"Are you having a baby?"

"What?" Emerson shrieks, making me laugh. "Just sit down."

Twisting the top off my beer, I sit in front of a fidgeting Jagger. "Spill it bro, worry isn't a good look on you."

Taking a quick swig of his drink, he looks from me to Emerson, and back again. "Em and I have been thinking of getting our own place together."

"Okay," I pause. "Not what I was expecting, but you know I have no issues with you here, and Em you're more than welcome to live here too. Come and go whenever you please."

"We know," they say in unison.

"But..." I raise my eyebrows expectantly.

"Dakota."

"What about her?"

"Sasha."

"Shit, Jagger, what the fuck is it?"

"Dakota is always going to come over, more so maybe, because I live here, and Sasha and you—"

"There is no Sasha and me," I cut him off.

"Exactly." Emerson squeezes his shoulders, and he sighs and slumps back in the chair.

"I'm going to leave you both to it. There's a shower and a bed calling my name." Jagger looks up at her hungrily, and she kisses him with a promise of what's to come. Forcing themselves apart, she struts away, and Jagger eats her up with his eyes.

"Just go with her," I tease. "We can finish this later."

"Nice try." He smirks at me, "She'll be waiting for me."

"I don't doubt that one bit."

"Do you want another beer?" he offers.

"Buttering me up?"

"Maybe." He makes a quick dash to the fridge and back, two bottles of beer before us, giving us both liquid courage.

"Look, Drix," he says calmly. "Your business with Sasha will always be your business, but you left to get away from her."

"I didn't leave to get away from her."

"Bullshit," he says, agitated. "Eight whole fucking months, and two seconds outside and nothing is better. Nothing is different."

"It doesn't matter, Jagger. Dakota is non-negotiable. I will endure whatever I have to, to see her. Whether you live here or not, makes no difference."

"I would never expect anything less, Drix." He shakes his head. "That's not what this is about."

"What's it about then?"

"I'm sick of seeing you in knots over her. She won't talk to me about it, neither will you, and it's killing me how much the whole thing hurts you both."

"I thought leaving would change things, but she couldn't even stand to look at me." My voice cracks and Jagger's face twists in anguish; there's no hiding how out of my depth I am. I don't have a solution and the notion that time heals everything is a crock of bullshit I can't wait around for any longer.

"You know." He runs his hand across the back of his neck before taking another sip. "She was a mess when you left." Strangely, his revelation calms me. Knowing I'm not the only one suffering. "She showed up here one night, eyes puffy, face drawn, it was obvious she'd been crying for hours. When she asked if Dakota could stay here for a week, I knew it was bad."

Images of me drinking everything in sight to the point where I couldn't remember who I was, where I was or what I was doing reminds me just how bad it really was. "Something happen?" he presses.

A loud whoosh of air leaves my mouth before I drop the bomb. "We slept together."

He doesn't say a word, so I continue. "It was here when we had that barbeque the day before I was heading out. It was our first, and last time."

"What?" he questions in shock. "You've known her your whole life, and never…"

"I've slept with a lot of women, Jagger, but none of them were her."

"Fuck." Confused, he repeatedly runs his hand through his hair. "I don't know—" He cuts himself off while shaking his head. "Well, what happened? How were you two after?"

His questioning is warranted. He wants more, a sliver of understanding of how we got to this complicated and fucked up finish line. I wish I could give it to him. To both of us.

Tipping the bottle up, I drain it of the last few sips remaining and place it down, empty, between us. I lean forward, look my brother straight in the eyes, and admit to the obvious, hard and painful truth. "It doesn't matter. It didn't change a single fucking thing."

two

SASHA

My shoulders sag as soon as I sit back in the car. The night is dark, and the air cold. The fogged-up windows hide me from anyone looking in and seeing me on the verge of a breakdown. I've had eight months to prepare. What the fuck am I talking about? I've had almost sixteen years to work out my shit, and I still can't figure it out.

The guilt. The wonder. The want. Damn the stupid fucking want. I've replayed every touch, kiss and ounce of pleasure he gave me for two hundred and fifty days, and it's been nothing but torture. I stupidly thought it was the goodbye we needed.

When I cornered him in the kitchen before he left, I thought I could rip the band-aid off and give in to the million fantasies he's starred in and send him off with well wishes and close the door on whatever it is Drix and I were. For good.

I was wrong. So fucking wrong. It wasn't needed. It was selfish, and I've been paying the price ever since. Every time I close my eyes he's there, in my thoughts, my dreams, like a ghost I feel him everywhere, but as usual, he's nowhere to be found.

When he left, the usual cracks in my heart were no longer small fissures I could control and fill. It broke. Whole chunks, dismantled, with serrated edges that could no longer be pieced back together. I thought I knew what hurt and loss was when it came to Hendrix, but it was really just an induction into the complete and dominating destruction of knowing what it would've been like to have him. Every single part of him, in every possible way.

The car door creaks open and Dakota steps in, placing a bag at her feet, she holds the gift with reverence on her lap. The drive starts in silence, as every part of me tries to recover from the small glimpse of Hendrix I allowed myself. Tonight he looked different, yet exactly the same. Freshly tanned, his body was languid, and relaxed. His eyes were a different story, the hate and hurt still burned as bright as ever. The only time he lets his guard down with me is around Dakota. I live for those moments. For years I've witnessed a boy turn into a man, to prove to the world that blood is thicker than water. For Dakota, he would lay his life down, and sometimes I don't know if that's why the pull to him is so strong. Going above and beyond, he put every injustice he suffered on the wayside for a gorgeous little girl that served only as a permanent reminder of all the reasons he and I never happened.

"Are you okay?" Dakota's voice pulls me out of my own self-sabotaging thoughts.

"Yeah babe, of course."

"You seem upset." I know how observant my daughter is. I don't know what she knows or what she thinks, but it's the one thing I refuse to talk to her about. She's a hopeless romantic and Hendrix is my secret for that reason alone. Knowing that my life would've been different if I didn't fall pregnant, is not something I want to touch her. The guilt, the pressure, the expectation, and the potential disappointment is too much for her heart and shoulders to bear. Either way, it's irrelevant and unnecessary. The only thing that would hurt more than a life without Drix, is a life without Dakota. She's my everything, and I would do it all again, no questions asked. A hundred times over, I would cry a million tears, and relive every painful moment to have her here by my side. Everything about her is perfection, her heart and soul are flawless. The personification of what love is and how it feels to be loved, she's been the bright days in my darkest times. She's my saving grace and the older she gets, the wiser and sharper she becomes. I can't keep much from her anymore, but this is a must. She'll make it her business to make sure her mother gets her happily ever after, and as much as I want that for myself one day, I want her to stay in the world of teenage drama and carefree living for as long as she can.

"I'm fine. I just wanted to make sure you didn't sleep late and you didn't overwhelm your uncle." With one hand still holding the wheel, I gesture to the wrapped box she's holding, "What did he get you?"

"I don't know." She shrugs. "He insisted I open it at home."

"How was your dad, and Em?" Purposefully I change the subject, knowing how much Dakota loves speaking about her dad. It makes my heart tighten in happiness and gratitude that as a family we're finally here.

"Dad tried to play it cool in front of Uncle Drix, but Em and I knew he'd been secretly counting down the days 'til he got home."

"Why am I not surprised. Your dad was always a vault when it came to his feelings," I explain. "He would do anything to avoid talking about them."

Rolling her eyes, she huffs in exasperation. "Aren't all boys like that?"

"What do you know about other boys?"

"Nothing." Her face flushes as she dips her head away from me.

"Dakota Michaels, is there something you need to tell me?" I ask animatedly.

"Nope." She shakes her head before pensively looking out the window. "Nothing worth mentioning."

Turning into the driveway, I switch the car off, and Dakota bolts to the front door, using her own set of keys instead of waiting for me. She's months away from being sixteen, I'm not surprised a boy has finally gotten her attention, but what I am surprised at is her hiding it from me. Usually she can't keep a single thought in, but I guess we all have our secrets.

"Dakota," I call out as I enter the house. Reaching her room, I push open the door and watch her; legs crossed in the middle of her bed meticulously unwrapping her gift. Curious to see what he bought her, I pad over to the edge of the bed and sit quietly.

"Holy shit," she squeals. She flicks through the pages of what appears to be a book of photos. "It's so perfect," she whispers. "If I made myself something this is exactly what I'd put together." She looks up at me with such adoration and delight. "Want to see?"

"I don't want to impose."

She cocks her head to the side, looking at me strangely. "Impose? You're my mum, you wouldn't know how not to impose."

"Excuse me," I scoff. "Are you saying I'm nosey?"

Her side eye game is strong, and I laugh. I shuffle up beside her. "You're right. Show me what he got you."

Dakota's little fingers turn each page. With such delicate precision, I watch her make sure she leaves no fingerprints on all the photos. "Uncle Drix showed me all the traditional tourist type photos over dinner, but I can't believe he knew these were the ones I would love the most."

"You've given him enough photography talks to last a lifetime, how could he not know?"

Mesmerised, she silently takes in the beauty of the hidden treasures of the world. While I feel Drix's love wash over me.

Stone alleyways, locals hanging over their balconies, people wearing traditional dress; the photos are powerful and hypnotic. They're also the exact parts of the world we discussed going and seeing together. A lifetime ago, he and I were going to travel to every corner of the globe. Close our eyes, point to the map, and fly.

Each photo has intricate details of different churches in Jerusalem, people at festivals in Rome, and an elaborate amount of street food in Barcelona. Hendrix brought fourteen-year-old me every inch of the world, and I fall. Farther. Deeper. Harder. Madly in love with him. As if the pain, the lies and the hurt never happened, I fall like it's the first time all over again.

"I wish I was best friends with those Michaels twins like you are," Bethany says. A little bit taller than I am, she rests her elbow on my shoulder and chews her gum loudly in my ear. Like every lunchtime, we're all circled around the edges of the handball courts while all the boys try and outplay one another.

It's a pit of teenage hormones, where the girls watch like vultures, and the boys perform for us. Showing off who's funnier, smarter, and stronger. But it's all a charade and completely unnecessary. All the boys know there's only two of them all the girls want; Hendrix, and Jagger. My boys. My best friends.

I've lived next door to Jagger and Hendrix my whole life. Hanging out on the decrepit streets of Sydney's South West, we became inseparable. Through the years the dirt and grime of our surroundings faded away, as we replaced them with a solid foundation of friendship, trust and loyalty. To everyone else they're deprived of positive influences; rough, misguided, and unpolished. To me, they're boys who stand proudly as men in spite of all that. They're my protectors; walls of steel hiding their truths, and gladly accepting the judgement, and labels; waiting for the moment where they'll show the world just how wrong she can be.

"I would be happy with either one of them," she continues.

Since we all came back from our summer holidays, school has been filled with endless amount of conversations of who's with who and who wants to be with who. Namely how the Michaels twins filled out, and how every girl is suddenly ready for them to be their first.

Looking straight ahead, I watch Jagger and Hendrix standing side by side, commanding all the attention around them. Animatedly they tell a story, throwing their heads back with laughter, and earning high fives and cheers from the boys who so desperately want to be them.

Their physical traits are too similar for anyone to notice how different they are. Jagger is night, and Hendrix is day. One can't function without the other, and together it's a beautiful blend of everything they have to offer. And the older we get, the more time we spend together the, harder it is to ignore.

"I'm going to talk to them." Bethany rights herself and starts adjusting her clothes; opening the buttons on her school shirt, allowing the top of her boobs to peek through. "Come with me," she murmurs, her mouth open, and a cherry flavoured lip gloss circling her plump lips. Bethany is like a dog with a bone. A gorgeous dog with a bone that's impossible to ignore. She can be obnoxious and annoying, but how she looks on the outside is enough to turn all the teenage boys inside out. She won't let her obsession go until she has a reason too, and for now, she's dug her claws into the idea of her hooking up with

either of them.

In the blink of an eye, irritation consumes me. "Do you have to chew so loudly?" I shake her arm off me and bend to pick up my bag.

"What's your problem?"

"Nothing," I lie. "I need to get to class."

Just like everybody else, I'm consumed by those damn Michaels twins. An unexplainable sense of protection and possession draws me to Jagger. A desperate need to keep his beauty to myself because nobody else deserves it. But with Hendrix, it's a selfish obsession. One where every day starts with applying subtle hints of mascara and lip gloss in the mirror. Wearing my hair a little different, my clothes a little tighter. A little shorter. For him, I'm desperate to cross lines and break out of the friend zone. But the fear of rejection and losing my best friend fuels my insecurities. It's a matter of what I want versus what's right.

Bethany walks toward him, and jealousy begins to simmer underneath the surface. I can't watch her flirt with him, and him enjoy it. I need to leave before my blood boils, and my best-kept secret overflows from my mouth and into the wrong ears.

Turning away, I head in the direction of my next class. Even though I'm unsure of what to do next, I do know it's beginning to impact our friendship. I've been avoiding him, instead of admitting my feelings, and it feels like the loss and change between us is inevitable.

"Sasha, wait up." My feet move faster. "Sash," he repeats, his voice closer, his body beside me in no time. "My legs are twice the length of yours, where do you think you're getting away to so fast?"

"Drix. Hey," I respond nonchalantly. "I didn't hear you."

He shakes his head and smiles. "Why do you even bother lying to me? What's wrong?"

I shake my head and shrug, for the first time feeling defeated that he knows me so well. We step together in silence. One second. Two seconds. Three seconds. *Eventually, a loud sigh leaves my mouth. Resigned by his patience, the words tumble out quicker than I'd like, the familiarity of telling him everything coaxing the truth out of me.*

"I just needed to get away from everyone, Bethany was talking my ear off and I wasn't really in the mood for it."

"Tell me about it, she was doing my head in too."

I look at him expectantly, wanting more of an explanation.

"She's just becoming so obvious."

My eyes narrow together. "Obvious?"

"Yeah, you know? The arm touching, the fake laughing. It's kinda hard to miss."

"Oh." I try to keep the disappointment out of my voice.

"The attention is nice, but it would be better from the right girl. Bethany's more Jagger's type."

Stopping outside my class, I let my backpack fall to the floor and lean my back on the rendered brick wall. He stands beside me, his shoulder brushing up against mine. My stomach flutters at his closeness. "I thought a girl that looked like her was everyone's type."

He turns his head toward me, his golden brown eyes holding my attention. "Not mine." His voice is steady and certain. His admission should mean nothing to me, and if he was anyone else I would read between the lines and take this moment as a hint; surrender to the attraction and tell the boy I'm in love with the truth.

I purse my lips together to stop the questions. Who is your type? What is she like? Could it be me? *Instead, I spin the conversation as far away from me as possible. "I don't think it matters who your type is, Bethany plans on wearing you down."*

"I'll just tell her I'm interested in somebody else."

"Are you?" I blurt out.

The side of his mouth rises in a slight smirk. "Maybe."

My gaze bounces between his mouth and eyes, and it takes all my restraint not to touch him. It wouldn't be unusual, but it doesn't come with the same innocence and freedom it used to. Biting the inside of my cheek, I lower my face and hide my shy smile.

"What's that look about?" he queries.

I shake my head, refusing to look at him. "I have no idea what you're talking about."

"Sure you don't." The bell signalling the end of our lunch break shrieks through the hall, breaking our moment. He pushes off the wall, and begins to walk backward, away from me, and to his next class. He doesn't say a word, but his stare might as well come with its own siren, because I hear it calling to me louder than any of the background noise that's begun to surround us. He calls out, and I have no choice but to give him the attention he deserves. "We walking home together?"

"When don't we?"

"I'm just checking, you know? In case something's changed."

He knows.

"Has it?"

He stops in the middle of the corridor like we're they only two people. "Only if you want it to."

He winks. My face heats up and my heart stops beating. Is he saying what I think he is?

three

HENDRIX

TWO MONTHS LATER

Casually, I push open Emerson and Jagger's front door. Slightly ajar, I figure they're inside busy settling in and setting up their new place. After spending all of yesterday packing and unloading both of their belongings from their separate houses, they're finally taking the next step.

A quick look around shows there's no one in sight. "Honey, I'm home," I call out into the empty space.

From behind the kitchen counter, a messy bun of blonde hair pops up, a familiar face attached. Nude, glossy, full lips pull up into a come-hither smile. Placing her hands on the caesar stone counter, she leans forward. Pressing her breasts together, her cleavage peeks out from the top of her loose tank. My eyes flicker between the glimmer of mischief in her gaze and her perfectly situated body.

A low whistle echoes throughout the room. "Well if it isn't sexy twin number two. Honey is home, and she would love a kiss."

My head shakes in disbelief as my chest rumbles with laughter. "The name's Hendrix."

"Oh, I know your name, but I like my name for you better."

Taylah is Emerson's best friend. Forced together a few times, all of our previous meetings have been fleeting, and filled with Emerson and Jagger drama. As first impressions go, she's loud, outspoken and unapologetically unfiltered.

She walks around the bench, and the full length of her body comes into view. Her black jeans grip her body tight, accentuating every curve perfectly. Her tank is shorter in the front showing off her porcelain midriff, and I kick myself for being too self-centred to notice what a delectable package she is.

Lifting herself up on the edge of the kitchen bench, she crosses her legs, and leans back on her hands, like she's waiting for me.

I oblige.

It's probably been nine or ten months since I've seen her, but this definitely feels like the first time. I'm not sure if it's because the environment is different, and the interaction isn't fuelled with tension, but I'm finding it difficult to keep my eyes focused on only her face. Stepping forward, I make my way to her.

Taylah's never hidden the fact she finds me attractive, and as my strides get wider and the distance between us shortens, I let the gorgeous girl with desire in her eyes inflate my ego.

Holding her seductive pose, she radiates confidence. My large frame envelops her, an arm on either side of her thighs; her expression refusing to waver at my closeness.

"So you're still crazy, I see."

The slightest hint of a dimple in her cheek appears as a small sensual smirk graces her face. "Me?" she questions dramatically, pressing her hand to the middle of her chest.

I raise an eyebrow at her antics, and she leans forward, bringing her mouth closer to my ear. "I prefer pandemonium in the flesh."

Her voice, those words, they travel straight to my dick. She knows what she wants, and after years of indecision, is there anything sexier than a woman who owns everything she is and makes you want it? "How about this?" I pull back and let my fingers discreetly graze her covered thighs. Her eyes follow the trail before we both look up at one another cravingly. "You can call me sexy twin, and I'll call you crazy."

"If you fuck as good as you look, you can call me anything."

She continues to stun me into silence. I have had my fair share of women throw themselves at me, but this isn't like that. It's not fake or attention seeking. There's no playing hard to get, mixed signals, or a worry about consequences. "Do you mean it, or do you say that shit for shock value?"

"Ha. There's always shock value, but it isn't intentional, it's just who I am."

"So, you want to fuck?" I study her face as the last word leaves my mouth, looking for a sliver of doubt or surprise, but she doesn't miss a beat.

"Are you offering?"

"Umm, should we come back?" Emerson's high-pitched voice breaks the spell, and we both turn to see her and Jagger in the doorway.

"If you don't mind us christening your house before you do, then yes, come back in a couple of hours." Taylah's responding to Emerson, but her eyes don't leave mine, and her smart mouth moves just for me.

"Hours?" Jagger scoffs. "Drix can't last that long." Straightening up, I turn away from Taylah and look at the two amused faces staring at us. Taking a deep breath, I give myself a small window of reprieve. A moment where I'm not thinking about taking her up on her offer and imagining us fucking in every room of Jagger's new place.

"Fuck you," I jest.

"While this thing between you all" —Emerson's hands gesture between the three of us— "is very entertaining, can you continue it later? The four of us are going to IKEA."

"Really, Em? You know that place scares me." Taylah hops off the kitchen counter, walks around me and plops her body on a piece of the dismantled couch. "You can only enter and exit one way. What's their fire safety plan, huh?"

"Don't worry Taylah, Drix will carry you," Jagger goads.

She looks up at me and bats her eyelashes. "Promise?"

Rolling my eyes, I stick my hand out for her to hold. "Come on, stop being so dramatic. There won't be a fire."

"I can't help it." She takes my hand. "Crazy and drama are cousins. And since—"

"You're crazy. I get it." I catch Jagger grinning like a smart arse, and I flip him the bird knowing very well what he's thinking. "Let's go," I say to nobody in particular. "I'm driving."

"Shotgun," Taylah shouts.

Yep. She's fucking crazy.

"Babe, do we really need two of these trolleys?" Jagger asks Emerson, pushing one in my direction and grabbing another one for himself.

"Yes, we need the extra one for Dakota's room. I want to make sure she has all the necessities before she comes over."

"She's coming over tomorrow."

"I know, so we better get cracking."

I mimic a whip hitting the ground in my brother's direction, getting him back for his joke earlier. He sticks his finger up at me and I laugh at how lucky I am to have this back with him. I'm comforted that time and age don't matter, he'll always be my brother and we'll always be in one another's life, no matter what the world throws our way.

The flatbed trolley jostles underneath my hands, and I see Taylah sitting right in the middle of it. Legs crossed, comfy as fuck. "What are you doing?"

"Sitting," she responds casually. "This is the only way I'm going to feel safe. If there's a fire, you'll just mow everyone down with the trolley while running to get us out."

"You're serious?"

"Come on sexy twin number two, you know you want to."

"Only if you drop the number two. I'm the only sexy twin."

"But you're identical," she challenges.

"You wanna ride with me or not, crazy?"

She smiles. No sarcasm, no seduction, just a genuine smile that lights up her whole face. "Well then, sexy, let's go spend Emerson and Jagger's money."

We follow Jagger and Emerson who are arm in arm, constantly looking up at one another, and kissing each other whenever they can, like the thought of not touching for even a moment is too hard to bear.

"They're ridiculous but adorable, right?" Taylah interrupts my thoughts, the scene in front of us playing on both our minds.

"I wouldn't call my brother adorable, but happiness suits him."

She turns her whole body, so she's facing me, her back to the rest of the store. "I can't imagine not seeing my brother or sister for that long."

"You have siblings?"

"No. Emerson is the closest thing I have to a sister and if I

don't talk to her once a day, my day doesn't feel complete."

Twelve years without my brother by my side, was probably one of the hardest things I've ever lived through, but I don't say it out loud. That's not who I am. I let others share their weight and burdens, but I don't share mine. I take what I've been given, and do with it what I can.

When Jagger went to prison, I learned the hard way what alone really meant. Doing the right thing by him meant I sacrificed a lot of me. He's my brother, I have no regrets, but while Jagger might have been missing out on life behind bars, I was out, free, and feeling as locked up as he was.

"You and Emerson that close, huh?" I ask, changing the subject.

"That close and then some. Before your boy here took up all her time, we were inseparable."

"Does that bother you?"

"What? That he takes up all her time?"

I nod, answering her question.

"Fuck, no. Look how happy she is." We both stop and watch them laughing at one another while they look at different bookshelves. Taylah brings her focus back to me, our eyes back on one another. "You're not the only one who can be selfless, sexy."

"She's going to love the way you've set up this room for her." Jagger and I are finishing off setting up the last piece of furniture

in Dakota's new room. Accompanying her new bed, there's a bookshelf, a desk, and a huge cork board that she can use to stick all her photos up on. It's missing her personal touch, but I know once she sees it, she'll do everything she can to make it her second home.

"I just want her to know wherever I go, she goes."

"You've been doing a great job, bro. She loves you."

"I still can't believe I have all this. I'm out and here with you, and Em and Dakota. It's almost been a year and it still feels like a dream."

"It's real. You've earned every bit of happiness you have. And this isn't the end, more will be coming your way."

"I couldn't have done any of this without you."

"Even though I think you're wrong, it doesn't matter because you're here. Right now. And that's what's most important."

A knock on the door sounds before Taylah's head pops in. "You guys down for pizza and beer or Chinese and beer?"

"Pizza and beer," Jagger and I respond in unison.

"God, how often do you two practice that?" she asks before walking out and shutting the door behind her.

Scanning the floor, I pick up loose plastic, nuts, bolts and whatever tools we used to assemble the furniture.

"So, you and Taylah, huh?"

"Me and Taylah?"

He punches me in the arm. "You were about to fuck her on my kitchen bench."

I smirk thinking about it. He's on the money, if we were alone any longer it probably would've happened. She was there. Sexy as hell, and willing. "What does it matter? It's not like I'm marrying the girl."

"Just remember she's Emerson's friend," he says, his voice serious, a complete change from the jokester he was seconds before.

"And?" We share a brain, I always know what's coming next, but I'm playing dumb. Purposefully leaving no room for misunderstanding, I want him to spell out whatever his problem is.

"Have fun but don't let it get messy."

"Messy how?"

"She's Emerson's friend and I don't want it to be awkward if you fuck her and run."

I clench my jaw in frustration, reminiscing about my time away when I didn't have to explain anything to anyone or worry about anything but myself. Moments like this, I wish I was still there. "While it's none of your business and hasn't been for a very long time, have you met Taylah? You think she's the type to let any guy treat her less than she deserves?"

"She'd probably cut your dick off."

"Exactly. I thank you for your concern, but I'm just going to do us all a favour and not go there. I don't need to end up in this situation with you."

"What situation?"

"The one where every woman that spends longer than two minutes in my presence is somehow attached to you and your life."

"I—"

"I don't want to talk about it, Jagger." I stand and scan the room, making sure the mess around us is cleared. "Forget I said anything." With my hands full, I make my way to the door. "Let's go drink beer."

"Drix."

"No. Beer. Please."

We step outside, one after the other, and the tension follows each of our steps. Emerson and Taylah's voices become quieter, acknowledging the change between us. The air thickens and I don't have it in me to make it better and play nice. "I'm just going to chuck all this shit in the bin outside."

"Drix," Jagger calls out after me.

I flip open the lids of the two bins by the side of the house, separating the shit in my hands between them.

"Drix," he repeats, his voice closer.

"I said drop it, Jagger."

"I'm sorry, just forget I said anything. It's your life."

Ignoring him, I head back inside. I grab my keys from the coffee table as I hear him call for me again.

"Hey sexy, you want to come pick up the pizza with me?" Taylah's standing there, her hands on her hips, her gaze, all-knowing. The strain between Jagger and I is obvious, and for whatever reason, she's trying to fix it. "Come on," she urges. "I didn't get to show off my singing skills the last time I was in your car."

I exhale in defeat. It's unfair to take it out on her. For the sake of her efforts and not wanting to be the one to fuck up a time where my brother should be happy and proud. I tilt my head to the door, and in complete understanding, she follows.

I hit the unlock button on my car remote, and we both climb in on either side. Pushing my foot on the brake, I press the keyless ignition and wait for the car to start. From the corner of my eye, I see Taylah fiddling with the car control screen. "What are you doing?" I ask.

"Drive to the pizza store. I got this," she demands.

Reversing out of the driveway, I throw a few glances her way as she concentrates intently on whatever it is she's doing. Soon enough she relaxes into the seat, and Tupac's "California Love" plays through the car.

"Is this the right song?"

She hits pause on her phone. "What? You don't know girls that like Pac."

I open my mouth and close it even quicker. I'm tongue tied, something that seems to happen often around Taylah. I shake my head and try and focus back on the drive.

Satisfied with my lack of response, she presses play and the well-known music picks back up.

Words from the first verse fall off her tongue with ease and conviction, like she's done this a million times. Her upper body starts to move, her movements matching the beat. She's dancing on the spot, living in this very moment.

I stop the car at the traffic light, and she twists to face me. She raps the whole second verse, watching me watch her, and never falters. The passenger window begins to slide down, and she starts singing into traffic.

With her back to me, I smile. Big. Impressed. Relaxed. The knots in my body from earlier begin to loosen, and the whole incident with Jagger is shoved to the back of my mind. The only thing I'm interested in, is what song she's going to sing and dance to next.

She's in her own world, and I'm nothing but a spectator.

Yep, she's fucking crazy.

four

HENDRIX

As the afternoon turns into the night, Jagger and Emerson's new place is all complete and ready to be lived in. With all their furniture set up, their kitchen unpacked and everything that makes a house a home in place, the next phase of my brother's life is ready for the taking.

When Taylah and I returned with food and beer, the fight between Jagger and I dissipated. Both having time to cool off, the rest of the evening went off without a hitch. Having indulged in dinner, Em and Jagger now sit on the couch, their bodies draped against one another, while Taylah and I sit in separate recliners, facing one another. With the perfect view in front of me, I have been watching her every move; the more the buzz of the beer settles throughout my body, the more obvious I become.

"Oh my God," she groans after looking at her phone. "Is that the time? I'm going to have to call it a night."

"I'll drive you home," I offer.

"There's no way you're driving her home," Emerson cautions. "Do you know how much we've all drank?"

"Fine, we can catch an Uber together." Right now, subtlety isn't my strong suit, and I'm too mesmerised by her to want tonight to end.

"Why don't you guys just stay here," Jagger suggests. "One of you can have Dakota's bed, and the other can sleep here on the couch."

"It's Sunday tomorrow," Emerson pipes in, looking at Taylah. "It's not like you have anything to rush off to."

"I have breakfast with my mother."

"Which you hate."

"Shut up, and stop being so practical."

Em claps her hands together and stands up enthusiastically. "It's settled then. You two figure out which of you is sleeping where, and I'll get blankets."

The living room empties out, Jagger following Em on her quest to make everyone comfortable. As quick as they disappear, Jagger returns with a pillow and some blankets, throwing them all on my lap. "I'll see you two in the morning."

"Thanks," I call out.

"Goodnight," Taylah adds on.

A quick wave over his head and he's gone to bed, leaving us alone for the third time today.

"I'm going to sleep out here and you can take the room."

"Sounds good." She untangles herself and rises from the chair. Off balance, she falls, landing straight back in the chair. "Shit."

In less than two steps, I'm crouching beside her, my hand on her knee. "Whoa there, crazy. Are you okay?"

"Yeah." Her cheeks flush with embarrassment. "It's been a long day, and alcohol and numb legs aren't a good combination."

"Here, let me walk you to the room."

"No. No," she insists, shaking her head. "I'm fine. Honestly." She places her hand on my shoulder, giving it a light squeeze. "Thank you, though." We stare at each other for two seconds too long, the alcohol-fuelled daze written on both our faces. I contemplate kissing her, knowing she wouldn't hesitate to kiss me back. But the way I'm feeling right now, it wouldn't be enough. She's a woman every man wants wrapped around his dick, but I'm not fucking her in my niece's bed and under my brother's roof.

Softly, she brings her lips to my cheek. "Night, sexy."

Stuck between stop and go, I watch her sway her ass into the bedroom. At the sound of the door closing, I hang my head and let out the breath I've been holding onto since the moment I thought about kissing her.

Unfolding the blankets, I lay them across the couch and put the pillow in place. Shucking off my jeans, I hang them over the arm of the chair and climb under the covers. With my arms behind my head, I stare at the ceiling, my mind replaying the day.

A habit I developed after Jagger went to prison, I reminisce on everything. When Dakota got hurt, I spent days and nights agonising over every conversation I had with Jagger and Sasha. Thinking about how I missed what and who he was involved with? I have always believed that if I wasn't so absorbed in my own feelings about the Jagger and Sasha mess I would have saved my family. Objectively I know my brother would have always done what he saw fit, but it doesn't mean that guilt doesn't sit deep in my chest, rising to the surface, teasing me of a life that could've been.

A door creaks open from behind me, the position of the couch makes me unable to see who it is until they walk past me. Long, toned, naked legs pass my head, and I have to stifle the groan that wants to leave my mouth. With no care in the world, she heads to the kitchen wearing nothing but her underwear and loose tank. Wearing lace, maroon underwear that cut across the middle of her arse cheeks, my eyes zoom in on the slight jiggle that happens with every step. She disappears into the kitchen, the sound of running water the only indication someone else is awake.

Her silhouette comes back into view, the lights that line the street breaking through the blinds, illuminating parts of her body. "No pants."

"Shit." She startles, her eyes finding me. "Give a girl a warning before you scare the hell out of her."

"Sorry," I say unapologetically. "Are you okay?" I ask her, brazenly eyeing her smooth skin.

"I needed water."

"And the uh...?" I flick my gaze up and down, from her head

to her toes, wordlessly asking the question.

"I don't know about you, but I don't sleep with jeans."

"What if Jagger was out here?" I challenge.

"I thought about it, but he's too busy fucking Emerson into the headboard right now. I figured the coast was clear."

"And me?" I can't pinpoint the need to constantly argue with her, but there's something about her that has me desperate to hear the sharpness of her tongue. Her no bullshit, full of confidence, sassy as fuck mouth.

"You don't seem to mind." She steps closer, her eyes glancing over to my jeans. "How about we pick up where we left off this afternoon." She takes hold of the edge of the blanket. "I can pull this off and we'll be matching."

I take hold of her wrist and pull her toward me until her face is only a breath away from mine. "You can tease all you want, Crazy, but we all know you can only poke the bear so much before he bites."

"Is that a promise or a threat?"

"I'm just saying, there's only so many times a grown man can say no."

"And there's only so many times a girl can handle rejection."

"You think I'm rejecting you?" I question, amazed she would think anyone would turn her away.

"I think you're overthinking this whole thing."

"Overthinking, yes. Rejecting you, no. And that's all on me." I lower my head and watch my fingertips trace patterns on the length of her thighs, goosebumps following my slow and deliberate movements. "But so you know, if we were anywhere else right now, I would've pushed you, me, and your barely covered ass back in that room."

"I guess knowing that will have to do then." Her forefinger and thumb take hold of my chin, as she tips my head up, our eyes now locked with nowhere else to go. She leans in and kisses the corner of my mouth. "Night Drix."

I watch her walk away, and into the room, my body missing her immediately. "Night Taylah."

Clumsy and deliberate noises come from the kitchen, stirring me in my sleep. A slow and steady hissing noise joins in, and the loud whistle of the kettle ensures there's no chance of me sleeping any longer. With each waking moment, I try to stretch the stiffness out of my body. Even though I'm grateful for my brother's hospitality, there's no way my body can do this again. Reaching over, I grab my phone to check the time. *Nine am*. Planning out the rest of my day in my head; a long, hot shower and a midday nap in my own comfortable bed are definitely on the cards.

"Drix, you want breakfast?" Jagger's voice travels, revealing he's the one causing a ruckus in the kitchen.

"Good morning to you too. How did you know I was awake?"

"I didn't. I just didn't care if you were asleep." He comes into view, skillet in hand, plating the scrambled eggs he's just cooked. "Are you having breakfast here?"

"I can't work out if you're kicking me out or asking me to stay?"

"Both. Dakota is getting dropped off here in two minutes to spend the day. Decide what you want to do." Ever since Jagger and Emerson explained one of the main reasons they moved out of my place, he and I have been in a better place. Our relationship is no longer muddied by the history Sasha and I share, honesty working better, the easy navigation allowing us to put our own personal needs first.

"I think I'll leave, I need to get home anyway, and Dakota and I have plans to meet this week after school anyway."

"You think she'll like the set up here?" he asks, insecurity and worry lining his voice. "I really want her to be as comfortable here as she was at your place."

Getting up, I grab my jeans from the chair and slide in one leg at a time. I put my phone, wallet, and gum back in my pockets. While buckling up the belt, I walk up to the kitchen bench, close enough to see Jagger perfect Dakota's breakfast surprise. "Come on man, we both know Dakota is going to love coming here. She loves anywhere you are, you know that." I swipe off a piece of bacon off the plate.

"Fuck off, I already offered you some." He moves the food out of my reach and heads to the oven. He fiddles with the temperature and puts the foil tray in, keeping the already cooked portion of breakfast warm.

"Seriously bro, that room, and letting her create her own space here…I'll be surprised if you can wipe the smile off her face."

He hands me a glass of orange juice. "Drink this and get the hell out of my house."

"With pleasure." I throw the cool liquid down and hand him back the empty glass. "Let me know how today goes, I'll talk to you sometime during the week, yeah?"

"I'll be down at your office on Wednesday, I'm popping in to see some of the boys."

"Sounds like a plan." As I head to the front door, Taylah steps out of Dakota's room, fully dressed. Her bag hangs across her body, the strap falling deliciously between her tits, while her arms are held above her head, as she attempts to tame her wild hair into something more manageable. I dip my head in her direction. "Morning."

"Morning," she mutters.

"You're awfully cheery this morning," I joke.

"I need at least two cups of coffee running in my veins before I'm ready for human interaction."

"Well, I'm heading home now, and with how much Jagger loves to talk, I think you're safe."

A gust of wind flies through the house as the front door opens suddenly, Dakota and Sasha bickering in the doorway.

"Dakota, I don't care whose house it is, you knock on the door." All eyes are on them, as they continue to argue, unaware they have an audience.

"I don't have to knock at home," Dakota argues.

"Because there's no chance you're going to walk in on me with somebody else at home."

"She's right you know, nobody wants to be subjected to what I heard last night." Taylah's interruption has Jagger holding back a smile, and Sasha scrunching her head in feigned disgust at Taylah standing before her. "Taylah. Hi. I didn't know you would be here." Her eyes flick between us, and she serves me a forced smile. "Hendrix."

"Sasha," I respond politely. Unknowingly we've all stepped back into the house, easing Sasha and Dakota away from the doorway and into the living room.

"Hey, T," Dakota calls out. Like old friends her and Taylah give one another a high five, reminding me that this isn't the first time everyone has met. "Where's Emerson?" She continues to walk farther in, stopping and rising on her toes to kiss me on the cheek.

"Hey kid," I greet, lowering my head, making it easier for her to reach me. With a spring in her step, she leaves the awkwardness behind, walking straight to Jagger and hugging him hello.

"Oh, everyone's here." Emerson's presence breaks the ice, as her eyes skate over everyone deciphering each person's mood. There's a suffocating silence that follows as we all stand in a self-imposed freeze frame waiting for what's next.

"Okay guys, breakfast is almost ready, who's staying?" Jagger's voice cuts through the tension and has everybody moving into next gear. Taylah speaks first. "I thank you all for your hospitality, but I need to get an Uber on the ASAP before my mum makes it to my place first and starts going through my things."

"My mum does that too." Dakota rolls her eyes, and a genuine smile spreads across Sasha's face. I let myself watch her in this unguarded moment, trying to remember the last time I saw her look so relaxed in my presence.

"It was great seeing you both, again." She fiddles around with her phone, organising a ride. It's on the tip of my tongue to offer her a ride home, but the words never form. "Okay, I'm going to get out of everyone's hair, and wait outside."

"Taylah, you know I'll drive you home. Cancel it," Emerson orders. Jagger looks at me, his stare telling me what I know I should do, but for some reason don't.

"I'll have to pay for half now regardless. It's no big deal. I want you guys to enjoy your first family breakfast."

Emerson untangles herself from Jagger, and heads over to Taylah, wrapping her up in a bear hug. "Love you. Thank you for yesterday, and staying over. I'll see you at work."

"Always," she replies, hugging her back. "Seriously, I have to go now." Pulling away from Em, she gives a lazy wave to Jagger and Dakota on the table and then looks over to me, her honey-coloured eyes find mine, and a look of wistfulness passes so quickly, I'm sure I've imagined it.

"I've got to get Dakota's bag from the car," Sasha pipes in. "I'll walk you out."

"Perfect." Expecting them both to walk out the door, I'm

dumbfounded when Taylah makes a detour my way, pressing her lips against my cheek, for all to see. "It was nice seeing you, sexy."

Oblivious to all the eyes on her, mine watch Sasha's turn from relaxed to confused and then hurt. She lowers her face, and I wait for my own pain to come. Guilt. Remorse. But all the familiar emotions are nowhere to be found, instead they're being replaced by the disappointment of not knowing for certain when I'll see Taylah again. I take hold of her hand before she walks away. "I'll drive you home," I blurt out. "I'll cover the Uber cancellation fee, too."

She looks down at my very loud and obvious gesture, then back at me, satisfaction making its way down her features. "It's okay, sexy," she drawls, the slight scratch of sleep lingering in her voice. "I think I can spare some dollars for you."

five

TAYLAH

"Sasha, you coming?" She looks like she just bit into a lemon as she follows me, and I can't work out why.

"I'll be out in a second," Drix informs me. "I need to talk to Dakota about our dinner plans this week."

"Okay, I'll wait for you at the car." Sasha follows me in silence, and while we've only met once, I don't remember anything being awkward or tense. It was very different from the vibe I'm getting off her right now. "How excited is Dakota coming to see Jagger and Emerson in their new place?" I ask, hoping to break whatever ice there is between us.

"She loves spending time with Jagger."

The statement is final, and I figure there's no point trying to prolong a conversation that isn't really going anywhere in the first place. "Well, it was good seeing you again."

I turn when an unexpected question stops me. "Are you and Hendrix together?"

"What?" I ask in shock. I don't want to say yes, but for some reason I don't want to say no.

"Inside," she says, pointing back at the house over her shoulder. "It looked like something was going on."

"Oh, that? That was nothing, we just had a few too many drinks last night celebrating Jagger and Em," I explain. "You know, you've known Hendrix a lot longer than I. You could ask him yourself." The tone of my voice is different, less friendly, more accusatory. But the solicitor in me knows better. Never give too much information away, especially when you don't know why they want it.

"I'm sorry," she backtracks, waving her hands in front of her. "It's really none of my business, I don't know why I even asked."

I don't know why she asked either, but I'm not stupid. There's always a reason. Women are complex beings, and one thing every other woman knows, is we rarely do anything without thinking about it first.

"Hey." Hendrix's voice finds us before he does. But by the way her eyes dart to the side, following his movements, alerts me to his presence anyway. "Are you ready to go?"

"Yeah, Sasha and I were done talking." Sasha turns her head away from us, and Drix tenses behind me. I think I now know what the issue is. I turn to face him, schooling my face to look less ruffled than I feel. "I might call that Uber."

"What, why?" With pretend confusion written all over his face, he looks between us, hoping nothing could've possibly gone wrong.

"Stay here with your family," I encourage.

"I can't stay here." His words are for me, but their meaning only makes sense when his eyes linger a little too long at the woman behind me.

Like yesterday, the impulsive need to pull him out of his sullen mood is instinctual. "Okay, let's go. I've got another song I need you to hear." The side of his mouth rises reassuringly. Looking back at Sasha I'm taken aback by her expression, a whirlpool of longing and pain staring straight at me. "I'll meet you at the car," I tell Hendrix, feeling compelled to give him and Sasha some time alone. "Um, it was nice seeing you again, Sasha."

She raises her hand in response, words failing her this very moment. I head to the car, and pray it's unlocked, itching to have distance from whatever this Hendrix and Sasha situation is. Pulling the handle, the door opens with ease. A black Hilux, Rogue, and what looks to be the most recent model; his car is all man. Just like him, it's refined, and sleek with an intimidating presence that only adds to the appeal. Trying to swiftly manoeuvre myself into the beast of a vehicle, I place one hand on the inside armrest and use my right foot on the car step. Using both as leverage I simultaneously push and pull myself up until I'm levelled enough to slide on to the passenger seat. Closing the door, I use all my willpower to not look up at their interaction. I don't want to be interested, I don't want curiosity to get the best of me. I don't want to care. I don't want to be sucked into a disaster waiting to happen.

I rummage through my bag for my earphones and then spend a minute or two scrolling through a playlist on my phone. I'm hoping to find the perfect song to transition me from what happened outside, to the drive home with Hendrix. That's what I do. I use music to fill-in the gaps, to speak when the words are too hard or awkward to find. It's always been my solace. My comfort. The edge off a hard day, or the soundtrack to a perfect moment. Whenever there's a significant time in my life, music is always the unyielding best friend. Holding my hand, getting me through.

By the time the driver's side door opens and Hendrix steps in, I'm already two verses and a chorus into "Shake it Off" by Florence and the Machine. I keep my eyes down and focused on the screen in front of me, pretending that the music playing in my ears has me entranced enough to not notice he's beside me, or that I saw Sasha lock herself in her car when she's supposed to be going back into the house with Dakota's overnight bag.

Fingertips shadow my earlobe, gracefully pulling at the earbud. Florence's voice disappears, and I'm left with no choice but to acknowledge the defeated expression written all over Hendrix's face.

"Can you sync it up through the car?" he asks, surprising me.

"Of course." I keep my voice as normal as possible, like his mood change isn't obvious, or how his slumped shoulders make him look like a young boy who's lost his way. "Do you have any requests?"

"Whatever you were bopping your head to will work just fine." I connect my phone to the car stereo, and the song picks up right where it left off.

"Here, let me put it up some." I reach for the volume, but his hand covers mine, pushing it away.

"I was kinda hoping you could do that whole sing and dance thing you did for me yesterday?"

Instead of being my usual self, I curb the sarcastic remark that would normally come out and tease him for lying about his enjoyment of my antics yesterday, and I restart the song, preparing myself to act crazy at his request.

"Okay, are you ready?"

He chuckles, "Am I ready for crazy?

I nod.

He turns away from me, his eyes darting straight to Sasha's car. The sound of the ignition mixes with the bass of the song. Once he checks his blind spots his focus returns to the hunk of metal that holds his secrets. He exhales loudly. "I don't think I'll ever be ready."

The heaviness settles between us. "That's okay, sexy, you get points for trying."

"Just pull up here," I direct. The car slows down in front of my house, my car in the driveway, which means my mum is inside, just as I expected.

"Is that your car?"

"Yes, my mum needed it. That's why I didn't have it at Emerson's. But look," I gesture between the two of us. "This would've never happened."

"This?"

"Yes. You and me in a perpetual state of talking about random shit, while really wishing we were naked."

"Really?" He drags his hand down his face, stopping over his mouth, clearly thinking before he speaks again. "I thought it was pretty safe on the drive home."

"Only because we were both busy distracting you from whatever went down with Sasha." My hand covers my mouth as I mumble a muffled string of profanities under my breath. "Fuck, I'm so sorry. I have no idea why that slipped out."

"Probably because it's the truth."

"It's also none of my business."

"You can't help what you saw, and whatever it is that happened before I got there."

"It was nothing, honestly."

He shifts in his seat to face me. "Don't lie now."

"I'm not."

"It's the one thing that's so refreshing about you." It's simple, but probably the nicest thing someone has ever said about me. My honesty has gotten me into trouble more times than I can count, and I was sure this was heading in that direction. "Can I ask you what she said?"

"What do you think she asked? She wants to know if the guy she's in love with is with someone else." He raises an eyebrow, perplexed like the idea never even crossed his mind. "Why are you surprised?" He doesn't answer, so I decide to push the situation even further. "Don't worry, I told her we're *only* fucking,"

His jaw clenches and I wait for an outburst. Something to show how he really feels, a hint at why he's so wound up about what went down, but as the seconds pass, whatever it is, festers. "Look, I might not have a filter, but I'm not an idiot. I didn't say anything to her," I huff, frustrated at his silence. "Besides the fact that I think it's none of her business, you seem to be forgetting there's nothing to tell. And," I continue to ramble. "If it makes you feel *any* better, she was so embarrassed she even let herself utter the question." He's twisted himself away from me, facing the front and gripping the steering wheel. I take it as my cue to leave. "Okay, that's enough for today. Thanks for the ride." Grabbing my phone, I open the door and jump out as quick as I can, my bag still hanging across my body. Getting caught up in this shit isn't worth the last few hours of my weekend. I slam the door only to be unexpectedly pushed back up on it.

"I'm sorry." He cages me in with one arm, the other hand pinches the bridge of his nose. "This whole weekend caught me off guard."

"The whole weekend?"

Both his arms are on either side of me now, his body covering mine. "Yeah. You and then Sasha. I didn't expect to enjoy your company, and I had hoped to avoid hers."

"Should I be offended you have really low expectations of me?" I ask feigning hurt. "Because that's not the first time that's popped up."

"Yeah, it's not the only thing that pops up when it comes to you."

"Look at you twenty-four hours in my company and those sexual innuendos are strong." A soft, coy smile materialises on his face, and he hangs his head to try and hide it. Standing straighter, my body forces him to look back up. "Don't get shy on me now, sexy. Tell me about how you enjoy my company."

"Let's just say it's been a long time since someone has piqued my interest as much as you have."

"And let me guess, Sasha is the reason why?"

He's silent, again. Unlike me, he thinks before he talks, which also means quiet time is often. I decide to cut him some slack, remind him I have no expectations when it comes to his past. "I know the answer, and contrary to what's going on in your mind, in this moment, I don't need to know about you and her."

"I feel like I should apologise for her attempt at interrogating you."

"There's nothing to apologise for. People in love do and say crazy things—"

He cuts me off, "She's not in love with me."

"Now who's lying?"

"I'm not lying," he insists. "It's not something I do."

"Then you're blind." I slip my phone in my back pocket, and place my hands firmly on his chest, putting us as close to eye level as I can. "I would bet my whole house she's in love with you."

"You'd lose."

"Pffft," I scoff. "I'm a solicitor. I never lose."

"With Sasha, everyone loses."

"You sound bitter."

"Just experienced."

Every revelation is another puzzle piece, and I'm forced to taper down the curiosity brewing within me. I'm torn between my natural need to want to know every morsel of every story, and the want to specifically know his story.

"And this got a lot heavier than I anticipated." He holds my hands and pulls them off his chest, hiding his in the front pockets of his jeans, subtly putting distance between us. "I should let you go."

"Yeah, my mum has probably turned my whole house upside down by now." I tilt my head toward the house. "I'm surprised she's not peeking through the window right now."

He turns, checking for himself nobody is spying on us. "What's she looking for?"

"Condoms, pregnancy tests, men's clothes. Anything to prove I have a life, really."

"She wants you to sleep around?" he asks, wrinkling his brow.

"She thinks I need male company, which she hopes and prays turns into marriage and babies."

"And you?"

"And me, what?"

"Do you need those things?"

"No woman is going to turn down a good dick every now and then." I never say or do anything for shock value, but watching his expression every time I say something unexpected is entertaining. "But I'm not that girl."

"What girl?"

"The one who needs to fill that void, or who has a five-year plan and has to cross everything off that checklist before she hits a certain age. I live every day the way I want because I can. Whether I'm alone in ten years' time with five fur babies, or married to a man that loves me more than I ever expected, and wants to fill our house with a soccer team of children, it will be what only I wanted, and I'll be happy."

The space he needed earlier doesn't seem to come into play as he pushes me back onto the car. Breathless and exposed from my little outburst, I struggle to regain my focus, but he uses it to swoop in and take control. He laces his fingers into mine, guiding my arms up above my head, the veil of pain and sadness that covered his eyes earlier has been lifted, replaced with nothing but unadulterated want and hunger. "I want to kiss you."

My tongue peeks out in anticipation. "So, do it."

"I can't," he says, a pained expression on his face. "I won't want to stop."

"Is that so?" I purr.

He pushes his pelvis into mine, his thick shaft pressing against his jeans, and into my stomach, answering my question. "I want to be able to give you that good dick you like every now and then, and I can't do that with your mum waiting."

"Right." The reminder of my mum has me looking behind him, scanning my windows, and making sure we don't have an audience.

"The minute she leaves," he continues. "I want you to call me."

"And then?"

My head falls back, and my eyes close as soft lips latch on to my collarbone. "Then we're going to organise a time where it's just you and me." He talks in between kisses, gracing the length of my neck, and stopping just below my ear. "Then I'm going to show you exactly how it should've gone the second you said you wanted to fuck." He nips at my earlobe and I fail, miserably at suppressing a loud moan, my imagination running wild at the visual he's created. He pulls back, releasing me so he can cradle my face in between his hands. "Me and you, crazy, we're going to rewrite the weekend."

six

HENDRIX

As soon as I walk through my front door, every knot in my body loosens. The good and the bad rolling off, leaving me to be alone and uninterrupted with my thoughts. Heading straight to the fridge, I pull out a beer and waste no time seeking relief in the bottle. I sink into the couch, take my phone out of my pocket, and put my feet up on the coffee table, in no rush to get back to the real world.

The drive home was a video loop of the last few hours. Taylah. Sasha. Taylah. Sasha. And repeat. Everything seemed to be okay until Sasha and I were in close proximity, and I immediately got caught up in her bullshit. In those few minutes she spoke to me more than she had in months, the words missing their usual smokescreen of niceties and pretence, replaced with inquisition and accusations that she hasn't had the right to in a very long time.

The possibility of finally moving on lit a fire within her that should've felt like victory, but all it did was ignite fury, disgusted with myself and how strong her hold on me has been. I've never dated long enough for anything to eventuate, my love and need for Sasha was always a reoccurring point of comparison. A standard that no one could meet. But today, for the first time in my life, I was able to see the other woman in the room, and I don't know how to process it.

I hopped into the car, my mind a mess, resentful that Taylah was watching me unravel, and then I saw her swaying in her seat, and lip-syncing the words to whatever song was playing in her ears, and I realised she didn't care, and I was grateful. The whole drive home she followed my lead, didn't press me with questions or coax me for answers, and I found myself itching to lay my secrets at her feet. Before I knew it, I was pushing her back up on to the car, turned on by her unfaltering certainty, desperate to bury myself inside of her, wanting to drown in her strength and courage.

My dick perks up at the memory of Taylah pressed up against my car, and I take advantage of my first night in a silent and empty house. Freeing my hands, I raise my shirt, unbutton my jeans, and drag the zipper down. Pulling my cock out of my briefs, I arch my neck back, and I close my eyes; letting the last twenty-four hours spin like a carousel wheel in my mind. I make a fist around my shaft and drag my hand up and down, working myself up, as I think of all the ways I would've had Taylah if I accepted her advances.

My release builds from my head to my toes, and I stroke myself faster, chasing the rush. My balls tighten, and quick, and fast ropes of come spurt on to my stomach. My body shudders, as I sag into the couch sticky, and sated.

It's not a solution to my problems, but it sure as fuck is a really good band-aid.

My phone rings as I step out of my bedroom, fresh out of the shower. Sasha's name flashes across my screen. Even though Jagger is around now to call me if Dakota needs something, old habits die hard, and I find myself answering the call. Pacing the length of my house, the uneasy feeling from earlier returns, my gut telling me I'm not ready for whatever bomb she's about to drop.

Milliseconds of silence pass before I decide to rip off the band-aid. "Sasha, what is it?

"I told you at Jagger's I'd call."

"And I told you not to bother." Rubbing the back of my neck, I feel the frustration within me switch from simmer to boil. "You asked me if Taylah and I were together, which I found out you'd already asked her, and we both gave you the same answer. So, what's left to discuss."

"You've been begging me for years to talk and now you're going to turn me away."

"Turn you—" Pinching the bridge of my nose, I take deep

breaths, trying to calm myself down, knowing if I don't shut this conversation down one of us will say something we will regret. Without an audience, the claws always come out. "That's right, Sasha. Years. Years, I've been trying and now you're ready, I'm supposed to just jump for you?" The air suffocates me, everything feeling too tight. My clothes. My skin. Every emotion adding an extra layer, determined to bury me alive. "Are you hearing yourself right now? Years I've put up with your indecisiveness and now you see a little competition and you want to stake your claim?"

"So, she *is*competition?" Fixated and stubborn she refuses to accept there's nothing going on between Taylah and me.

"I don't know what she is, but I didn't know you were in this race."

"I've always been in the race, Drix."

"Are you fucking kidding me right now?"

"Why are you so surprised?"

"Why?" I cut myself off for the second time. *Deep breaths.* "You've spent years avoiding me, telling me it's too complicated, or how Dakota finding out about our past is just too much for you to handle, and now Taylah shows up, and you're what? Ready to make this work?"

"No, it's not exactly like that." Her cryptic rejection still hurts, and I hate that my mind is telling me to argue with her, not wanting to be at her mercy, but my heart still waits for the day where she'll agree, unconditionally to be mine.

"Enlighten me. Please."

"Before you left..." The sentence doesn't even need to be complete to conjure up the images, the feelings. Every touch. Every taste. "Since then I can't handle the thought of you with anyone else."

I find myself in my bedroom, my aimless pacing leading me to the place where it all happened. Weak knees, sagging shoulders, the strength to fight with Sasha has been decimated with a few words and an avalanche of memories.

"So explain this to me, you can't handle the thought of me with anybody else, but you're still not sure we should be together."

"I just saw you two together, and I know I'm losing you."

Along with my body, my voice loses all its fight. "You can't lose something you never had, Sash."

"Let me come over," she interrupts.

"No," I say with forced conviction. "You might not be able to watch me with someone else, but I can't let my hands touch you, my mouth taste you, and my heart fall deeper in love with you, just to watch you walk away from me one more time."

"I need you."

"No, you don't. You're just jealous," I say, trying to simplify our circumstances. "And jealousy makes you say and do crazy things. It always has. I'm not going to be another addition to your list of regrets. Not this time."

"I regret a lot of things in my life, Hendrix Michaels, but you are not one of them."

"After all this time, Sasha." I shake my head to an empty

room. "I find it really hard to believe you." I let out a long, low sigh, defeated, again. "I'll talk to you later."

"Dr—"

I end the call. I just can't go around in circles anymore. I'm dizzy. All we do is dig up old dirt, shifting it around, never leaving the secrets, lies, and betrayals alone long enough to settle.

I know it wasn't all bad, but as the years pass the good has become harder to remember.

Leaning against the brick fence, I wait for Sasha. Anxiety floods my insides, my palms sweaty in anticipation. Tonight is the night we stop dancing around our feelings and I tell her I want her to be my girlfriend. She's been my best-kept secret. Even from Jagger.

But over the last month, I've been a bit more forward. Her shy smiles and flushed cheeks spurring me on, proving I didn't imagine the attraction between us. Tonight, we're going to go to the party, together,*and after so much worry and uncertainty, she's finally going to be mine.*

I hear her voice before I see her. "Mum, I'm going out with Drix. I'll be back later."

"Okay, don't forget to check in."

"I'll send you a text."

"Can you just call, you know I can't work out how to write back."

I turn as the screen door flies open and she bounces her way outside, effectively ending the conversation between her and her mum. Time stands still as I watch her, remembering the little girl she was, running with the boys, to the young woman she is today.

The one all the boys want.

I've stood in this same spot every day of my life, my brother and my best friend by my side. The three of us living in the moment. Too young to live for more than today. But as I stare, mesmerised by Sasha, I realise this is the first time I've ever thought past right now. I see a world of endless possibilities, a world that's brighter, and full of opportunity. A world I want with her as my girl.

I could bet a million dollars that you won't find many boys my age declaring forever. Like Jagger, they're all too busy fumbling around their virginity, desperate to feel more than their own hands. Jagger is the impulsive one out of the two of us. The confident guy with the ladies; the Michaels brother that could flirt before he could talk. I've always been content not being the centre of attention. And when it comes to girls and sex, I didn't have a reputation to live up to, or a desire to start one.

I'm not rushing. I'm not there yet, and Sasha and I, together, definitely haven't reached that stage. She won't be my first kiss, but there's no way anybody but me will take her virginity.

If she'd had sex with anyone else, I would've been gutted, and have to get over it. However, knowing she hasn't, makes me want to stake my claim like a ridiculous caveman, so all she'll ever know is me.

Hunched over, I lean on my forearms and watch her jump off the last step, and head my way. She tilts her head, her eyes focused on me and the space between her eyes creasing with curiosity. "Whatever's got you thinking so hard, is going to make us late."

Chuckling, I place the tip of my index finger between her brows and pretend to rub away her worry. "We're going to be late anyway. I have something planned."

"What do you mean?" she asks, looking around like she'll find a clue. "Where's Jagger? Isn't he coming?"

"I told him to meet us there."

Her frown returns. "So, it's just going to be me and you?"

I clear my throat, nervousness getting the best of me. "Is that a problem?"

"No," she gestures with her hands. "Of course not. Just a surprise that's all."

Refusing to feel discouraged, I wipe my clammy hands on my jeans, slide them into my pockets and lead the way.

The walk is silent, our bodies close, but our minds definitely running on different wavelengths.

"Drix, you're being weird. What's up?"

"We're almost there, and then I promise, I'll explain everything."

We settle into a more comfortable silence as the walk progresses. As we come up to our local park, I find my balls and slide my hand into hers. "This okay?"

Her breath hitches at the contact, and a bashful smile builds as surprise sinks in. "Definitely." I stop us directly in front of the wooden tree house, positioned next to a huge, and very out of place blue-gum tree. It was solid, stable, and older than the two of us. "Why are we here? You know how much I hate this place."

"I do, but, I have my reasons." Squeezing our hands together, I raise my fingers to the top of her forehead and trace the scar I know sits just behind her hairline. "Remember when this happened?"

"Ughh, how could I forget. I was so sure I was going to die. There was so much..."

"Blood," we say in unison.

"You know, when they kept you in the hospital overnight, Jagger threatened to knock me out cold if I didn't calm the fuck down and stop worrying about you."

"You were worried?"

"Fuck, yeah. I was torn between wanting to sleep at the hospital or tear limbs off all the kids that forced you to swing off that rope."

The summer between our thirteenth and fourteenth birthday, we spent every afternoon here, watching the sunsets, and running amok with all the neighbourhood kids. Besides the treehouse, the park was littered with childlike play equipment. It was beaten down, more of a symbol of our neighbourhood, than having any actual functioning use. The only thing we all obsessed about was the swinging rope. We never knew how it got there, or why it never frayed, or why the thick branch it was wrapped around never bent or broke under our weight. It was our constant. The simple thing that made moments in our childhood seem like that they could, and would last forever.

"It was dumb, and I should've known someone as uncoordinated as me was going to chicken out, lose my balance and fall."

"You want to try it with me now?" I ask.

"What?" Her eyes widen in fear. "Hell no."

"Come on. It's just you and me."

"What if the same thing happens?"

Softly my thumb and forefinger take hold of her chin, tilting her head up to face me. With as much truth and sincerity as I can muster, my words simultaneously ask and tell her, "You think I'm going to let anything happen to you?"

A wooden box on stilts, the treehouse is as rickety as ever. I'm not always the best with words, and maybe the idea is better in theory than it will be in practice. But I want Sasha to know how serious I am about this. I can't take one more day of us sidestepping around our feelings. I need Sasha Allman to be my girlfriend, and I'm not taking no for an answer.

"Climb up," I order. One foot at a time, she trudges her way up the ladder. Looking up, my intention is to make sure she doesn't trip or stumble, but my concentration falters as I stare at her tight, denim covered arse.

It's bittersweet when she makes it to the top, and the view disappears, but I follow, eager to get to the end part of my plan.

The rope hangs from the branch, but rests inside the treehouse, on a rusted metal coat hook. Reaching for it, I explain to a stiff and scared Sasha that we're going to swing off the ledge, and land in the sandpit together.

She glances between me and the thick strands of twisted synthetic cord. "I don't think I can do it."

"Here," I say, ignoring her and grabbing both her hands. I line them up, one on top of the other, and meticulously close each finger until her skin is blotches of white and red, and she's holding on for dear life.

I fit my own hands in between hers, now a pattern of knuckles lining the length of the rope. "I'm going to pull us back, and swing us out, all you have to do is let go when I tell you."

"I don't understand why you're making me do this." Her voice trembles and a sliver of guilt settles in my chest.

I don't waste any more time trying to convince her it will be okay. The quicker I get this over with, the quicker it will all start to make sense. Pulling against the rope, I get us in position. "I got you, Sash. Just let go when I tell you."

Without any further warning, my legs run us off the edge. We cut through the wind, my eyes focused on her while her eyes are squeezed shut. The sandpit is directly underneath us, ready to catch our fall. "Now."

I wait for her to let go, wanting to take the full brunt of our swing backward if she decides she can't go through with it. But she does.

A shrill laugh fills the air, and together our arms flail, as our feet search for landing. A loud thud signifies our safety back on solid ground. "You did it," I state through ragged breaths. "I told you, you could."

She launches straight into my arms, a show of affection I didn't anticipate. I drink in the scent of her, in no rush to let her go.

"I can't believe I let you talk me into that." With her head nestled in my neck, her words a mixture of murmurs and heavy breathing. "Now. You have some explaining to do." She unlatches herself from me, and I miss her instantly. "What's all this about?"

I shake out my limbs as if I'm preparing for kick-off in a big game and psych myself to plunge into a speech I've recited to myself more than a million times. But the long-winded speech I'd planned seems unnecessary and too time-consuming. Instead, I shocked us both blurting out the life-altering truth. "I'm in love with you."

"Whhhaat," she stammers.

"I brought you here, to tell you this was the place I realised my feelings were changing. And the last few months have been torture keeping secrets from you." My anxiety fades as the words leave my mouth, the cliché of the truth setting you free, becoming more relevant than ever. "I've dropped hints, but it just feels like wasting time."

"Wasting time?"

"I want you to be my girlfriend, Sash. There are no two ways about it." I step to her, clutching her face in my hands. "I won't do another day where everyone doesn't know we're together."

"Do I get a say in this?"

"No, you'll try to tell me why it's a bad idea, even though I've seen how you look at me."

"You're so sure."

"Nobody knows you better than I do, Sasha. Together we can overcome our fears. I just showed you that," I say, glancing at the treehouse. "Say yes."

"How can I say no?"

"I want to hear the word." I move closer, my lips a breath away from hers. "Say it," I whisper.

"Ye—"

My mouth devours her answer. I swallow the one word I've wanted to hear from her for so long, The kiss gets deeper, and I let her reservations spill into my mouth, gladly, taking them, showing her they have no place between us. Our tongues tentatively seek one another out, finding comfort, and warmth. While our hands awkwardly roam, feeding into the inevitable rush of pleasure swimming through us.

Finally, she surrenders, her body melting into me. Like two pieces of a puzzle, we fit. Like we were supposed to, just like I always knew.

seven

SASHA

I toss the phone on the passenger seat and pound on the steering wheel three times. I can't believe I'm parked outside his house, and he just hung up on me.

Sitting here is irrational and so out of character, but after today, I couldn't let the last thing I see be him driving away from me, to be alone, with *her*.

The one and only other time I'd met Taylah we were watching Drix and Jagger play football for a Y*outh off the Street*s fundraiser, and she didn't hide how attractive she found him. She's Emerson's friend, Dakota was there, and he isn't my man, so I seethed internally and let the day pass. It's not like I can't see how gorgeous he is, he's perfect, grown up to be everything a woman wants her man to be.

But the bottom line is he isn't mine, and for the first time in a long time, the reality of that is sitting heavy on my heart. I feel insane, conflicted, hurt, and defeated. I know I'm the reason we're here. Every fight, every rejection, almost every reason we're not together can be traced back to me. And for some unknown reason, I'm still here acting like I have a right to dictate how the rest of his life goes.

I step out of the car, slamming the door like it's my own personal enemy, and head straight for his house. My knuckles rap at the door loudly. Only seconds have passed and I'm hammering at it again, even harder.

"Who is it?" he asks, his voice close, and the consequence of my decision on the cusp of evolving.

"Drix. It's me." The door swings open with more force than necessary, and the sight of him in front of me has every single one of my senses on full alert. Even with his frustration and anger on full display, he's still so impressively beautiful. His hair points every which way, like he's been running his fingers through the top for the last five hours. His eyes are tired. Dull and deflated, and I can't help but feel responsible.

"Sasha?" He looks back at his bedroom then back at me. "We just got off the phone."

"I was already outside," I try to explain. "I told you, I wanted to see you."

Closing his eyes, he looks down, his chin to his chest and shakes his head excessively. "This is *not*a good idea."

"I know that, but I'm here now." I step closer to him, and he steps back. The rejection stings, but it seems wrong to turn back now. "Can I come in?"

He presses his back against the door and gestures for me to walk through. Grinding his teeth, I know he's anything but pleased.

I stand in the middle of his living room, battling the unwanted feeling, forcing myself to get through the discomfort. "Drix. I know I'm not welcome he—"

"Don't lay the guilt on from the get-go." He slams the door closed, effectively interrupting me. "For as long as Dakota has spent time here, you've always been welcome. But she's not here, which doesn't make you unwelcome, it just means I can't work out why you're here." He folds his arms across his chest, and glares at me, his eyes hard and cold. "Do me a favour once and put me out of my goddamn misery, and tell me why you're here."

My chin begins to tremble, his resentment hurting more and more as each second goes by. I open my mouth, only to close it, fear getting the better of me.

"Tell me," he urges.

"I'm so fucking lost, Drix." The tears fall without warning, the confession a painful reminder of how conditional I've allowed my own happiness to become. "I'm miserable like this."

A weak laugh leaves his mouth, as he hangs his head, and covers his eyes with his hands. He looks back up, his pained and confused expression mirroring mine. "And whose fault is that?" he asks. "Because it ain't mine."

"Don't fall in love with her."

His eyes widen, the words surprising us both. "What are you saying, Sasha?"

The tears fall harder. "Just promise me you won't fall in love with her." Habit has us walking toward one another, the small gap between us a stark contradiction to the reality of our situation.

"You're talking about a woman I barely even know."

"But I know. I saw the way she looked at you. The way she could look at you." I wrap my arms around his torso and rest my cheek on his chest. He stiffens underneath my touch, warring with himself whether to hug me back or not. "She'll love you right. She'll love you better. She'll give you a life that I can't."

He kisses the top of my head. "I don't have any more pieces left of my heart you can fucking break." Coupled with his heartbreaking revelation he holds me tighter and gentler than I deserve, igniting a rush of tears that become uncontrollable to contain.

"I'm sorry, Drix," I hiccup through sobs. "I'm so sorry. I just need a little bit more time."

"You're telling me fifteen years wasn't enough?"

"I can't explain it."

"Well until you can." He moves back, and lowers his head, quickly pressing his mouth to mine. He moves painfully fast, and I'm unable to get my fill of him. "I can't hear how you don't want me anymore."

Holding his face in my hands, I hold him tight enough, so all he can see is me. "I want you. I want you more than I can put into words."

"I don't believe you."

"Kiss me. Kiss me so I can show you just how much I want you." He closes his eyes and shakes his head, and the switch in me flips. No longer able to bear his disappointment in me, I throw myself at him. I let my lips do the talking, and his can't help but speak right back. It's an old and tired conversation, one we've had many times. Promises we've made a hundred times, promises we've broken a thousand more.

The rest of my body buzzes back to life with every swipe of his tongue. We melt into one another and the walls between us break down. He takes hold of my arse, lifting me up and guiding us to the couch.

We sit, me straddling him with my hands still holding his face, desperate not to lose him to reality. His dick offers a warm welcome as my hips instinctively rock against his hard cock. I'm on the very edge of giving in, wanting to fall into him, and fall apart for him.

He's gripping my hips so tight, moving me back and forth, when all of a sudden, he stops.

"Drix?" I call for him and try to bring him back, my voice breathless, shaky and full of fear.

Resting his forehead on mine, he doesn't say a word, and it's the beginning of our connection severing slowly. I feel the loss of every sense, more hurtful than the one before.

"Sash," he whispers into the empty room. "You need to go."

I hear him, but neither of us moves.

"When I can't hear you and see you and have the chance to taste you, I can't want you." His eyes break my heart before his words do. Conviction. Determination. Resolve. "And I can't want you anymore."

Two streets away from his house, and I pull the car over and park on the side of the road. I don't know if my body is breaking down or trying to fight back, but I can barely breathe. My head is heavy, my lungs feel like they're collapsing, and my throat is closing up on me through every uncontrollable sob.

I've done this, cry tears over Hendrix Michaels more times than I can count, but this, right now, constricted by the four doors of this car, it feels final. Like for the first time in my whole entire life I won't be able to dust off my knees and pick myself up off the floor.

The worst part is these tears are my own fault. When I can't seem but to be anything but reckless with his heart, how can I hate him for protecting it? For doing what's right, even when it hurts. It's what he's always done. Be the bigger person. Be the better person.

He ignores my flaws for the most part, and all I do is let them be the reason why I will never give us another chance. It's a self-imposed punishment because I don't deserve him. I didn't when every boy gave him shit in high school for how much he loved me. I didn't when I accused him of not loving me enough. I didn't when I gave my virginity to somebody else, and I hammered the last nail in the coffin when I fell pregnant with his brother's baby.

I'm fucked up in the most clichéd of ways, and I broke Hendrix and I enough times just to watch him pick up all the pieces whenever I needed him to.

He's done more for me than I'll ever do for him, and it took a woman with hair like mine, a body like mine, and an appreciation for how fucking beautiful Hendrix is, just like me, to finally accept that I'm losing him.

I lean my head on the headrest and wait for the remaining tears to leave my body. I need to get home. I need to drink a whole bottle of tequila and sort out my fucking life. Before I know it, my daughter is going to leave me, and our home, looking for her own happily ever after, and every excuse I've ever had to avoid living my own life won't be valid anymore.

Starting the car, I pull out and head home. Faster than is legal, I do the twenty-five-minute drive in fifteen. I fly through the door and remove every piece of clothing off my body as I make my way to the kitchen. By the time I'm sculling my second tumbler of tequila and grapefruit juice on ice, I'm standing in nothing but my bra and underwear, begging for the numbness to hurry up and takeover.

Pouring the third glass, I take myself and my liquid dinner to my bedroom. I set everything on my bedside table and walk into the back of my walk-in wardrobe and pull out a box I've kept hidden for a very long time. I take another large gulp of my drink before I open Pandora's box.

I scatter the letters written in multi-coloured pen and covered back to front in adolescent handwriting, all over my bed. I find my most prized possession and bring it to my nose.

The paper is thick and green, folded 'til it can't be folded anymore. Sprayed in Hendrix's sixteen-year-old cologne, it smells exactly the same way it always has. I open it and a small thin gold band falls out. I slide it down my left ring finger, but thirty-year-old me has bigger fingers, and it stops just before my knuckle.

Tracing the letters of each word, I read the note that became the beginning of the end.

Sasha,

I have a question for you.

When we get out of this place, will you marry me?

Drix.

"How can you be so sure?" I ask him, my face hurting from how wide my smile is right now.

We're laying in the sandpit at the park, staring at the stars. A place that has become our safe haven ever since the night Hendrix made me come back here.

"I just know. I've always known." My head rests on his inner arm while his fingers play with the strands of my hair. I hold the letter he used to propose and sniff it excessively, loving the scent of Hendrix all around me.

"And you don't think we're too young?"

"I think we're too young to do it right now, but not too young to know it's right. and by the smile on your face, I think you agree." He pulls his free hand out of his pocket and a ridiculously girly squeal leaves my mouth as he places the petite, delicate gold band on my ring finger.

"You got a ring?"

"It's nothing fancy, but it's real, and I saved hard for it."

He's so proud, it makes my heart want to burst. I rise out of his hold and turn to face him. "You don't need to buy me gifts, Drix."

"I know, but I want to, and if I can, I will."

My hands on his chest, I lean down and kiss him quickly. "Drix."

"Yeah?"

"I can't wait to marry you."

"I can't wait to marry you either."

The kiss starts off slow, as usual, but this time, the love passing between us feels as if it could set the world on fire. I've never felt so much for one person. When he touches me, I don't want to stop, and when he kisses me I pray it never ends. And now the flutters at the pit of my stomach, make it impossible to put the brakes on it because I know where I want to go next.

But I'm scared.

I love Hendrix. So much, I want to make him happy in every single way. It's what boys want and I want to go to the next level with him, but I feel if we go all the way, we'll have nothing else to look forward to for the rest of our lives.

I want to keep things moving and keep things interesting, but I don't want to rush.

We have forever, right? What's the rush?

"I can hear you thinking, babe. Stop."

"I'm not," I lie.

"You are? And I'm happy to wait."

I hide my face in his chest. "How did you know?"

"One day you'll realise that there's nothing about you I don't know. We will get there, and it will happen exactly when it's meant to." He shifts slightly so my chin is resting on his chest and he can hold my stare. "Do you trust me?"

"Always."

SIX WEEKS LATER

The loud shrill of the bell echoes throughout the school, and the end of the year is finally here. Hendrix and I have been waiting for the school holidays for what feels like forever. To be able to see each other every day and not be bogged down with all the school work we've had creeping up on us lately.

Hendrix and I made a deal, we wouldn't let our relationship interfere with school, so we wouldn't jeopardise our future. Drix wants out of here, away from his mum and away from his past. Me? I said I would follow him wherever.

My relationship with my mother was as good as any teenager's could be. I told her what she needed to know, and she reminded me not to grow up too fast. I was an only child with a dad I didn't know or care to find.

That was the one thing Drix and I had in common, deadbeat dads. Their lives were too important to include us, or their dislike for our mothers was too much of a hurdle to ignore. Whatever their excuses were, they soon didn't matter. We just want our future to be fresh, bright, and everything two hardworking kids deserved.

"So, you and Drix going to have sex this summer?" Bethany asks as we pack up our books.

"What is your obsession with me and Drix?"

"You bagged the hottest guy in school and you're such a prude about it all. You're never together, too busy studying." She sits on the edge of my desk, hands behind her, chest protruding out, trying every which way to make sure everybody knows how attractive she is. "And if you're not careful, he's going to leave you for another girl. A girl who would be glad to have sex with him."

Bethany was supposed to be my best female friend, but since Hendrix and I got together, her jealousy has spiked my insecurities to an irrational and uncontrollable level.

It's Bethany who should be my punching bag, but I don't want to give her the satisfaction of knowing the shit she spews actually bothers me. I keep it all locked up and pour my heart out in my diary before I go to bed. I write about how scared I am he'll realise how mediocre I am compared to all the girls who are desperate for his attention. How I feel forced to sleep with him to keep him, and the one thought that scares me the most, fucking this up and losing the most important person in my whole world.

I should talk to him about the way I feel because I know he'll ease my fears, but instead, I listen to Bethany and pick a fight with Hendrix. He doesn't know why and he begs me to explain it to him, but I don't. I brush it off, push it deep, and force it away. Until the next time.

"Hey, Sash, what's with the face?" Jagger comes up behind me, sliding my backpack strap off my shoulder and carrying it for me.

"You don't have to do that."

"Besides the fact that I've been doing it forever, you're my brother's girl, I got to take care of you when he's not around."

I pinch his cheeks like he's a little baby, our sibling type relationship strong. "Thank you. What would I do without you?"

"So," He flicks my fingers from his face. "You can't hide from me, you going to tell me what's up or not?"

"Just girl shit. You know how we are. One day we're friends and the next you're wondering why."

"Sometimes I wish I was a girl so I could know what it's like to have tits for a day."

"That's so helpful Jagger, what would I do without your input."

"Be less entertained that's for sure." He pulls an LCM Bar out of his pocket, unwraps it and stuffs it in his mouth. No bites, all in one go. "You ready to go home?" he asks with a full mouth. "Drix is waiting and he'll be blowing up if I'm not delivering you to him in record time."

"I'm not a package."

"Whatever, I just do what he asks because I am a great brother."

"Shut up, and let's go." He salutes, and I nudge him in the shoulder. "You're ridiculous."

"I know."

We walk through the corridor, heading toward Block B, where Drix had his last science class for the year. I could pick him out from any crowded place, and this time it's no different. Unfortunately, it's not just him that I see, and my body physically freezes, but internally my blood is boiling.

"Sash." Jagger looks back at me, standing there, far enough behind him that the gap between us is obvious and awkward. "Are you coming?"

I stand there numb, unable to talk. Bethany has her hands all over Drix, and I can see him trying to dodge her, but in my mind, it makes no difference. All I can hear on repeat is her telling me he's going to leave me for someone else. Someone that will have sex with him whenever he wants it. Someone. Just. Like. Her.

"I have to go."

"What? Why? What's the matter?"

"Jagger, I have to go. Don't follow me, and don't tell him I saw him."

"Sasha. It. Is. Nothing."

I run off, ignoring him calling after me. My heart is crushing even though my mind knows better and is screaming at me to calm the fuck down. I don't. I run as fast as I can and begin to plan how I'm going to break up with Hendrix.

I'm never going to be the girl he needs, and the quicker he finds out, the better.

"Knock knock." Hendrix leans on the open doorway of the treehouse. His shoulder pressed up on the worn wood, his arms crossed like they're protecting his chest. His heart. "You going to let me in."

"It's a public place."

"I don't want to impose on your personal space. Especially since you ran away, to get more space." In less than two strides he's standing beside my sitting form, making me feel even smaller than I already do. "What's up?"

"We need to break up."

"What the fuck?"

"I saw you with Bethany today."

He lets his body clumsily slump down until he's next to me, our shoulders touching. "And?"

His voice is harsh and hurt, but I stick to the plan. "She's better for you than me."

"What are you talking about?"

"She would have sex with you tomorrow if you want it."

"Why are we talking about this again?" He buries his head in his hands and growls, "I've fucking told you I don't care."

"All guys care."

"I don't. I don't. I don't," he shouts. "We just admitted our feelings. We've been happy. I've been happy. We have the whole summer ahead of us. Fuck. I told you I want to marry you."

"I know. I know," I cry. "But that is so far away from now. Who

knows what will happen between now and then, and who we'll meet, and who we'll want."

Bending his knees, he rests his arms across the top and tilts his head to the side, to look at me. A sheen of tears cover his eyes, and I realise I'm making the biggest mistake of my life.

"I don't know what's gotten into you," he whispers. "But I fucking love you, Sasha. I'm going to give you whatever stupid space you need to get over this ridiculous bullshit that's going through your head." He gets up and walks away from me, each step another crack in both our hearts. "But in two days, you better be on my doorstep, because I have the best life planned for us, and I can't do any of that without you."

eight

TAYLAH

Throwing my laptop bag on my desk, I kick off my heels, and flop back into my desk chair. It's hump day and pretty much the end of everyone else's work day. Grateful to be out of court, even if it means overtime in paperwork, I grab a pen and begin to organise my to-do-list.

"Oh hey," Emerson calls out, stopping mid-stride. She's got her bag on her shoulder, ready to go home. "I thought I was going to miss you again. How was your day?"

"Wish it was better."

"That bad, huh?"

Covering my eyes, I take a few deep breaths and stop myself from having a mini-meltdown. As much as I love my job, some days the unfairness of the world hits me a little too hard. There are too many kids who need protecting and too many restrictions on how much support I can give them.

"Why don't you worry about this paperwork tomorrow? We can wind down, have a few drinks and dinner across the road."

Looking at the paperwork that surrounds me, I mentally calculate how many extra hours I'll have to put in this week to finish it.

"You know you want to," Emerson teases.

"You're right. Fuck it." I toe the inside of my heels, slipping the rest of my feet in and stand up. I do an awkward shimmy on the spot, straighten up my clothes and grab my handbag. "Let's get this show on the road. My favourite chicken schnitzel is waiting for me. See you, bitches," I call out to an empty office, before joining Em in an empty elevator.

"You letting the future husband know you won't be home for dinner?"

"He's not my husband," Emerson retorts. Finishing her text, she drops the phone back in her bag, her attention back on me.

"Don't act like you're going to be marrying anyone else." She smiles, and I know she's imagining herself in a wedding dress, walking down the aisle to her man. If I didn't love her so much, I'd probably make fun of how romantic and cheesy her life has become.

"He wasn't going to be home tonight anyway. He stayed back at the *PCYC* with Drix, they're training some of the kids from the youth centre. Boosting up his volunteer hours."

"How is that sexy brother of his?" I keep the tone of my voice as neutral as possible, playing it cool. Like I haven't been thinking about him since he dropped me off at home on Sunday morning.

"I actually thought you would know, I haven't spoken or seen him since you guys left on Sunday. Tonight is the first time Jagger has seen Drix since then too." The conversation stalls as we concentrate on crossing the road, and getting seated in the bistro-style establishment as quickly as possible.

Leading us straight to our favourite booth, Ben, one of the regular waiters, pulls out his mini tablet, ready to take our order. "The usual ladies?"

"Yes, please Ben," Emerson responds. We've been coming here for the last five years, only changing our orders when the menu itself has changed.

"Can we just get an extra side of fries," I add. "I'm going to need some carbs to soak up that second bottle of wine I plan on drinking."

"Right on top of it, ladies." He slips his stylus in the front of his shirt pocket before giving us a slight nod and walking back to the kitchen. My eyes move from his retreating form to find Em raising her eyebrows at me expectantly.

"What?"

"I'm just waiting for you to tell me what happened with Hendrix after you left."

"What made you think something happened?"

"You looked like the drooling emoji all weekend."

"Well," I sigh, dramatically playing up the story for

entertainment purposes "As true as your observation is, things got a little too complicated a little too quickly, and it just confused the fuck out of me."

"How?"

"Try the red neon sign flashing the letters S-A-S-H-A."

"I had my suspicions something went down when she hightailed out of our place, even after agreeing to spend the day with us."

Ben comes back with our wine glasses, pouring us each more than the normal, one standard drink of Sauvignon Blanc, he's required to. I bat my eyelashes at him and raise my glass as if I'm about to make a toast. "Ben, my love, you know me so well. It's only fair that I marry you one of these days."

He chuckles while filling up Emerson's glass. "As soon as the dick doesn't do it for me anymore, you'll be the first to know."

"I can't wait." I wink at him as he leaves, and catch Em rolling her eyes at me. "You're just jealous you don't have a Ben."

"That's definitely it." She takes a sip of her wine and my actions quickly follow. "So, are you going to start the story or not?"

"I always wondered why you never worried about Sasha and Jagger being together. I mean, they had a kid together, and that's a bond you won't share with anyone else, you know?" My fingers slide up and down the stem of the glass, as I use Emerson as my own personal sounding board. "But then when I saw the way she looked at Drix, it all started to make sense." She nods, and it's obvious that none of this is a surprise to her. "And when she asked me if something was going on between me and him, I realised just how complicated drooling over him might actually be."

"Wait, what?" She grabs my arm in surprise. "She confronted you?"

"Yep. It wasn't a full-on accusation, but it also isn't something you ask someone you barely even know."

"Did you tell Hendrix?"

"He walked up just as the conversation finished, but the tension was inescapable. Between her and I and her and him."

"Honestly, it's better if you don't get caught up in that." Ben arrives, the conversation pausing in his presence, as we make room for him to put each meal down on the table. "He's not really into anything serious."

"Thanks, Ben," we say, veering off the Hendrix topic for a split second.

"Who said anything about serious?" Grabbing my cutlery, I start cutting up my panko crumbed chicken schnitzel. "Sex doesn't mean I'm tying myself to him."

"I just don't think anything can happen. He's a great guy, and you could actually like him," she says in between bites. "But there's so much shit between him and Sasha, I just don't see how sex is worth the risk of a head fuck."

"What is it between them anyway? Are they exes?" Remembering how little he spoke about what happened, but how wrecked he was from seeing her, I anticipate a huge breakup.

"I only know Jagger's version, but even that has a twelve-year hole in it. Obviously."

"You still didn't answer my question."

"They've never been together as far as I know."

"That makes no sense." My brows furrow in confusion. "The way they were looking at one another.... Fuck, I don't even know how they can stand being in the same room together when they're feeling that way." Wanting to get as much information about their history as possible, I press on. "So they fell in love when Jagger was on the inside?"

"No. They've been in love since they were kids."

"But Dakota?"

She takes a long sip of her wine before dropping a curveball of epic proportions. "How would you feel if the love of your life had a kid with someone else. Your brother nonetheless."

"How did you never tell me this? Why would she do that?" A million different scenarios play out in my head, thinking of a teenage Drix looking even more shattered then he did over the weekend.

"There are three sides to that story, and I don't think we'll ever know all of them. What I do know is everybody is different and what's forgivable for one person isn't for the other."

"So, he won't forgive her, but he'll pine for her."

"I'm sorry I don't know more about this." Placing down her cutlery, she folds her arms and lets them rest on the table. "But my priority is you and Dakota and Jagger. There is so much pent up shit between them, it's dangerous." She reaches for my hand, giving it a light squeeze. "And I don't want you caught in the crossfire."

A huff of frustration leaves my mouth; at the situation, at being indirectly told what to do, and because of my impulsive need to do just what I want anyway. "I get it. I do. But he gave me his number, and it's just sex."

"Taylah," she chides.

"I haven't had good sex in a really long time," I whine. "Do you know how fucking sexy he is?"

"Actually," she smirks. "I kinda do."

"You bitch," I shriek, throwing a french fry at her. "I've heard you and Jagger, and I bet Drix could fuck me from here to next Sunday. Why would you deny me that?"

Em gives her head a slight shake. "I know you're going to do whatever you want to anyway, and if this were any other guy, you know I would be waiting to hear all the sexy details. But this time." Her tone takes on a seriousness Emerson has never used with me before. "If you plan on using that number, *please*be wise about it. For your own sake."

Emerson and I shelve the conversation as we get through our meal and the two bottles of wine. While the night helps wash off the grime from my day, Drix still sits at the forefront of my mind.

I think about him the whole way home, his number in my phone taunting me. I make a pros and cons list of all the reasons why I should and shouldn't call. The list is fairly equal, yet Sasha's name in the cons column holds more weight than any other of my bounds.

I'm not an insensitive bitch, and I'm empathetic for both of their heartache, but there's also a physical pull between him and I that I'm not sure if I want to walk away from.

If I'd known any of his history with Sasha, for Emerson's sake, I would've pulled back from him this weekend. In front of everyone it was sexual banter at its finest, but every time we were alone, it felt like something more.

When it comes to my career I am nothing but straight-laced, focus and goal orientated, but when it comes to my life outside the courtroom and away from all the injustices I can't fix, I live with reckless abandon. Usually listening to my own instincts, I jump head first and think later. Life experiences teaching me to regret nothing. Everything is a lesson waiting to be learned, and even if I was to get hurt, every now and then it might be worth it.

Showered, and relaxed, I jump into my bed and turn the television on. Flicking through *Netflix,* I stop at a new young adult movie I've already seen a thousand times and let it play in the background while I attempt to fall asleep.

Just as my eyes begin to give in to the heaviness, my phone vibrates on my nightstand. I groan loudly into the empty room, kicking myself for not switching it to do not disturb mode.

Punching in my passcode, my eyes adjust to the light. A message from Emerson lights up the screen.

Em: *I'm feeling really guilty about tonight.*

Looking at the time, I figure whatever it is, is playing on her mind, because she never sacrifices sleep time for late night chats.

Me: *It's late. What are you talking about?*

Em: *Drix*

Another message follows seconds after.

Em: *It's none of my business if you want to call him.*

Me: *It's not that big of a deal Em, we can talk about it tomorrow.*

Em: *I know, but you're a grown woman who can take care of herself. No matter what the outcome is.*

Me: *I appreciate that, more so that it's 11pm and you're up.*

Em: *LOL. Jagger got home late and I waited up for him.*

Me: *Waiting up for the dick. Good job, boo. I hope you got off at least twice.*

Em: *He just got out of the shower. Might make it a trifecta.*

Seeing as she'll be occupied until further notice, I don't bother writing back. Instead, I take her messages as approval and pull up the number, I had almost given up on using.

I agonise for a good ten minutes, typing and retyping the text. In the end, I settle for something witty and fairly closed. No questions, and no expectations of a reply.

Me: *I figured the three-day rule was bullshit and decided to message right before it was up. Sleep well, sexy.*

Debating on whether or not to switch my phone off and sleep, a message comes through quicker than I expect.

Hendrix: *I've been waiting for you to text me.*

Me: *Three days is hardly a long time.*

Hendrix: *Long enough when I've been jerking off to the very thought of you every single one of those three days.*

My insides coil at the image of him fisting his cock, the words on the screen enough to suck the air out of my room. My pulse quickens, as I take deep, long breaths. My fingers finding their way dangerously close to my underwear.

The phone vibrates in my hand, another message coming through.

Hendrix: *Cat got your tongue?*

Two can play this game, sexy.

I call him.

"Oh, so you *can* talk," he says sarcastically.

"Of course I can, it's just really hard to text with one hand."

"One hand? Where's th—" I hear his mind tick over, my innuendo registering. "Where's your other hand, Crazy?"

I click my tongue. "A woman never tells."

Low and gravelly, he asks, "Are you thinking about me?"

Yes

"Maybe"

"Let me stay on the phone with you."

Yes

"No. I'd rather have you drive yourself crazy imagining it."

"Meet me after work tomorrow."

Yes

"I'm busy for the next week," I lie. Tonight's warnings still playing devil's advocate in the back of my mind. "You might have to jerk yourself off for a little bit longer."

"Don't leave me fucking hanging, I want to see you."

Me too

"Sorry, sexy."

"Crazy," he growls, sounding hoarse and needy.

"Night."

Despite wanting to drive him crazy, I end the call and read back the text that started it all.

"Long enough when I've been jerking off to the very thought of you every single one of those three days."

Fuck. Me. Hendrix Michaels is going to set my body on fire, and I have no doubt I'm going to enjoy the burn.

nine

HENDRIX

It's Friday and I have never been so happy to see the back of a working week. Sunday night was a complete write-off. Instead of an early night to set me up for a good Monday morning, I drank until the numbness took over my body and my mind. Until I couldn't feel, until I couldn't remember, until darkness was my only companion. I made sure that I would feel so shitty every time I thought of Sasha, there would be nothing but bile and revulsion, because anything before that was a fantasy land, and I *need*reality. I need it quick. I need it to hurt, I need it to be honest with myself, and more importantly, I need *it*to be happy.

Monday arrived with a vengeance. Physically, I welcomed the fog. It provided a temporary relief from how shattered and destroyed I felt on the inside, but my brain had to work overtime to compensate for the sluggishness. Especially when an email lands into your inbox before you've had your morning coffee telling you your whole site and program is being audited.

The whole process is equivalent to getting all your teeth pulled out. Working with teenagers as a youth worker has been my calling for as long as I can remember. There's something so fulfilling about being able to help someone who would otherwise fall in between the cracks, and not in a self-righteous way, but more in the privilege of watching someone so vulnerable accept help and want to do better for themselves. Even if they don't know how important those first simple steps will be in their future, it's the effort that is life-changing. That's why I do this job. It's the one thing that makes the paperwork, the politics, and all the injustices, worth it.

Governed by the Department of Youth and Community Services they always love to surprise us with random file checks. Especially when we're in the process of requesting funding for our program to be extended for another three years. Every single kid has a file, more than three hundred clients, and every encounter documented. It's probably our fault they're not always up to date, but you always think you have time, and before you know it, time's up. So, it's been a crazy week, and I've earned the right to a drink, but after Sunday night, I don't think that's the answer.

What I do think will have my week ending on a high, is Taylah. I didn't think she'd come through, and after a heated discussion with Jagger at footy practice, I was pretty sure my life would be made up of fleeting moments where I wondered where she was or what she was doing.

Repeating his earlier sentiments about fucking around with Emerson's friend, he decided to remind me of the lifetime load of baggage I have with Sasha. Like I could forget. And even if there was a moment I did, the universe is ready to shove it right back in my face.

Not even forty-eight hours since our first text and she's got me in a constant state of arousal. Every second message is laced with sexual tension, every other one is me asking when she's free.

I want to fuck her. More than once. And if there's any way I can make it happen, I will.

Leaving the office a little later than everyone else, I climb into my car and call her number. It's the end of the week, and I've got energy to burn.

Four long rings pass before her muffled voice answers the call. "Hello."

"Taylah?"

"Hold on a second."

"Hey." With the background hustle fading into nothing, her voice comes through much clearer. "Sorry about that, I just had to find somewhere quieter."

"Where are you?"

"Central Station. Just waiting for the train home."

My eyes flick to the clock on my dashboard. "Overtime?"

"Ha," she scoffs. "Is it still called overtime if you don't get paid? I don't usually get out any earlier than seven, but when the words on all my paperwork began to blend with one another, I decided I'd had enough."

"Week from hell?"

"How did you know?"

"Must be the season." The conversation goes silent, and I can't pick whether she's uncomfortable or shy, but I proceed to get to the bottom of it anyway. "So, I was calling because I thought we could upgrade from the texting. Maybe have dinner, and you can tell me about the week from hell."

The pitch in her voice rises. "You want to eat dinner?"

"Well, everyone's got to eat."

"Right."

Shutting down the conversation for a second time, I figure I've got nothing to lose by pressing her to tell me what's got her so tongue-tied. "Taylah. Just spit it out."

"I thought this was just sex."

I laugh, grateful her unfiltered mouth is back. "Can I not feed you first?"

"I'm not opposed to it, it just wasn't what I was expecting." The sound of the train conductor announcing the next train interrupts her explanation.

"Care to share what you were expecting?"

"I don't know, less clothes." She pauses. "Dinner seems kinda intimate."

"Intimate? Crazy, intimate is when my face is pressed up

against your pussy. This is just food."

"Fuck. Drix," she hisses.

"What? You don't want to tease me right back like you have been every night."

"Let's just say you're lucky there's a platform full of people standing around me right now."

"Is that right?"

"Don't underestimate what I've got stashed up my sleeve."

"My dick's hard just thinking about the possibilities."

"And people say I'm the one who doesn't think before I talk."

"I can't help it, you seem to be rubbing off on me."

"And I am not walking into that one."

"Seriously." Putting our bold and brash conversation on hiatus, I try and convince her once and for all to meet up with me. "Let me pick you up from the station. We can go somewhere close and talk about work. Keep it light. Keep it casual."

"I can do that. I'll just text you the time the train pulls up, and where the easiest place to meet is."

Relieved she isn't shutting me down, I happily oblige.

Crazy: *Train arrives at Meadowbank Station at 7:26. I'll be at the Thai restaurant directly across the road by 7:30. See you soon*

The drive to Meadowbank isn't quick. Arriving five minutes late, I walk in and spot her sitting cosily in a corner booth. Just as I'm about to reach her, the waiter slides in beside her, catching us both off guard. Blonde, blue-eyed and slightly shorter than me, his lean frame angles into her. Annoyed that he's eating into my time with her, I walk a little faster, hoping to catch her attention. Unfortunately for him, he notices me first, taking it as his cue to swiftly slide himself away from her.

As he moves, her gaze follows, green eyes settling on mine. She offers me a coy smile and the smallest wave. While the confidence fuelled side of her personality is intoxicating, nervous Taylah is an alluring rarity.

She stands to greet me, and I enjoy the sexiness of her corporate outfit. From head to toe, I admire the curve of her breasts, peeking through her elegantly unbuttoned shirt, and accentuated by her high-waisted skirt. Down to her tight arse and toned legs, her heels are a wonderful addition to my own little fantasy.

"Sorry, I'm late." Pressing my hand to the small of her back, I lean in and kiss her cheek.

"That's okay. I had company."

"I noticed," I say, turning my head in the direction of the waiter. "I bet you can't go anywhere without someone trying to hit on you."

"It doesn't happen that often." Her eyes veer off to the side, proof she's lying.

I catch her chin between my fingers and bring her eyes back to mine. "I call bullshit."

Her shoulders lift in a slight shrug, as she takes her seat back in the booth. The same waiter comes back with menus, nodding at me with a tight, and unimpressed smile as he hands it to me.

"What's good here?" I ask, blatantly ignoring him.

"I usually get a Prawn Pad Thai, covered in peanut sauce."

"Sounds good." I push the menu away without even giving it a second glance. "I'll get that then."

"Are you sure? I kinda put that dish together, and it's not really for everyone."

"I'll take my chances." The guy from earlier returns, pen behind his ear, and notebook in his hand. "Do you want me to order the same for you?"

"No." She waves her hand in front of her and then addresses the waiter. "I would like a bowl of Tom Yum soup, please." Her face turns back to me. "I had a really late lunch at work."

"No problem." Collecting the menus, I interrupt his continual appraisal of Taylah and rudely shove them under his nose. "Thanks. We're done here."

"I'm right here," I say, shaking my head. "Could he be any more obvious?"

"Excuse me," she says, the sass returning to the tone of her voice. "He can look all he wants, we're not together."

"Right now, we are." Wanting to attach myself to her in any

way possible, I'm unfamiliar with the sense of competition and jealousy coursing through me. She's not mine, and I'm not hers, but the frustration and need building in the middle of my chest to have her, hints otherwise. "Why don't you tell me about your week from hell. I bet you mine rivals it."

"No," she groans. "I don't want to talk about it yet. You tell me yours."

"Well. Wait, do you know what I do?" I ask, realising the sense of familiarity between us doesn't actually mean we know a lot about one another.

"Jagger and Emerson have mentioned it."

"How nice of them," I say sarcastically. "Do they talk about me often?

She shakes her head while twisting an invisible key at the seam of her mouth, insinuating her lips are sealed.

"Whatever." I put my hands up in defeat. "I don't care anyway."

"I'm sure you don't," she teases. "Now stop stalling and tell me what happened at work."

"It's not that exciting," I start. "But we're getting audited at the end of this month, which is a pain, but it's almost impossible finalising all the paperwork when I've spent all my extra hours making sure my clients are staying out of trouble."

"I fucking hate when they spring that shit on you," she says in understanding. "Expecting it all to be up to date because your job only consists of paperwork."

"Every time it happens, I tell myself to be more up to date so

I don't go through the same shit next audit. But alas, I'm really talented at being extremely unorganised."

"It's definitely one of the shit sides of the job." She pulls a laptop bag in the air and points to it. "That's the reason I'm not staying back every night, I'm taking it home with me."

We sit through a meal, and order dessert, talking about all the things we love and hate about our jobs. I knew what she did for a living, but I forgot how close our circles ran.

I also didn't realise how much I like hearing her talk. About anything.

Specialising in family law, she knows all about the type of children I work with, where they come from and how hard the system has to work to make sure they don't get lost. In turn, I know how hard it is to be responsible for visitation rights, kids without parents and parents losing their kids.

It's a constant battle between wanting to save everyone and not being able to save anyone.

"Do you ever think you'll leave Legal Aid and go private?"

She skates her top teeth across her bottom lip as she mulls over my question. "I never say never, but right now, I'm happy and content. I get to have all the things I want for my life while doing something worthwhile for somebody else's."

The conversation hasn't turned to sex once, and I find myself enthralled, wanting to learn all the things about her. How empathetic she is. How much she has to give, how little she feels she needs to take.

A loud yawn leaves her mouth, and she rushes to cover it. "Shit, I'm so sorry."

"What are you apologising for?"

"Some days my inner old lady shows, and my body wants to be in bed by nine p.m.."

"Let's call it a night."

Apologetic eyes stare at me, and I feel compelled to clarify that being attracted to her doesn't mean I can't appreciate a good meal and great conversation. And if I'm honest, I think I needed this more.

"Taylah." I place my hand over hers, keeping her focus on me. "Thank you for light and casual."

"The food and company were pretty great, weren't they?"

I stare at her, because I don't want to look anywhere else. My eyes travel over every part of her, grateful the night took this turn. "Can we do this again some time?"

"I'll see if I can fit you in my schedule."

My phone rings, ruining the moment, and Sasha's name appears on the screen, adding salt to our wounds. I don't know how Taylah feels about Sasha, but I know she isn't stupid. There isn't a moment I can have without a reminder of her, and any progress we made just left the building.

She drags her hand from under mine. "You better get that."

"It's probably Dakota," I throw out, looking for a plausible excuse. "She sometimes calls off her mum's phone."

"Sure."

I've lost her.

Years of habit mean I can't let it ring out. "Hello."

"Uncle Drix."

A large exhale leaves my body, as Dakota's voice answers instead of Sasha's "Kid, what's wrong with your own phone?"

"I went over my data plan, so I'm trying to save money."

"You almost gave me a heart attack." I try to get Taylah's attention, but she looks everywhere but me. "What's up?"

"I'm just checking you're coming tomorrow."

"Of course I'm coming, when do I not show up."

"Never. I just like to check in."

"We're all going to be there," I assure her. "Are you sure you're okay?"

"I'm good. What are you up to tonight?"

"I'm having dinner with a friend." Taylah's body stills at my response. "I've got to go, okay? I'll see you bright and early. Get some sleep."

My favourite waiter brings the bill placing it in front of Taylah. She opens it, and slips her credit card in, just as I wrap up the phone call.

"Love you, Uncle Drix."

"Love you, too, kid."

I drop the phone on the table with a thud, and take hold of her credit card, handing it back to her. "What do you think you're doing?"

"Paying for dinner?"

Dragging my wallet out of my back pocket, I throw some cash in the leather holder and wait to hand it back to the waiter myself.

"I could've paid."

"I know."

"Dakota okay?" she asks, giving in to curiosity.

"She wanted to make sure I was going to make it to her soccer game tomorrow."

"She plays soccer?"

"She does every extracurricular activity her school has." I beam with pride at the beautiful young woman she's growing up to be.

"Do you always watch her?"

I nod, because it's the truth. Anything she has ever needed I've made sure she has.

"You treat her as if she's your own." It's an observation. One that scratches the surface of my deepest secrets. One that needs no confirmation from me. "You're a good man Drix,"

Unable to meet her eyes, I look down at the table. "I try."

ten

SASHA

With our picnic chairs set up along the sideline, Dakota's biggest fans, Jagger, Emerson, Hendrix, and I are here cheering her and her team on, hoping they win this game, and make it to the quarterfinals.

Seated in a row, Jagger and Emerson sit in between Hendrix and I; playing as our usual buffers. We used to be able to co-exist, but lately being around him is everything my masochistic heart wants. Every time we're together, it's just another layer being ripped off, exposing what I've been trying to keep hidden for years.

I feel like a balloon. Each year that's passed I fill myself up with shame, humiliation, and disappointment, but now I've finally reached the part where the balloon can't hold it together anymore. And I'm so close to bursting.

The halftime whistle blows, the score nil all, and a bunch of fifteen and sixteen-year-old girls ready to rip each other apart. For such a non-contact sport the mood and undertone is ruthless.

Jagger and Hendrix huddle with the team, pretending they know anything about soccer when really they just like to scare all the other parents from falling in the trap of sideline coaching.

"Want some?" Emerson offers me some dried apples, and I turn my nose up at them in disgust.

"I really don't know how you eat those. The texture in your mouth is gross."

"They're not that bad," she argues. "And they're so healthy."

"Please, just eat unhealthy shit like the rest of us."

We laugh with ease, a friendship I never thought I would want, yet somehow, I cherish dearly. So caught up in my own bubble I didn't know I needed an outsider. Someone who I don't have a history with, someone I can start fresh with. Someone who isn't afraid to hurt my feelings when I need to get the fuck out of my own head.

We both watch Jagger and Drix walk side by side across the field. Guaranteed our thoughts are very different, but we get caught up in their presence all the same.

"Can I ask you something about Hendrix?"

"I don't know how helpful I'll be, but my ears work just fine."

"Is he with your friend Taylah?"

She uncrosses her legs, only to cross them again. "The truth?"

"Please."

"I don't know if there's anything going on *right* now." She turns her head to face me, her expression unreadable as her sunglasses cover her eyes. "But there's a very high possibility that something may happen between them in the future."

"Why am I even surprised?" I murmur to myself. "He's a catch, any sane woman would jump through hoops to have him."

"So are you insane?"

"Huh?"

She raises her shades letting them sit on the top of her head, her eyes boring into mine. "So, why are you not with him?"

Unruffled by her frustration, I answer her honestly. "I don't deserve him."

"Maybe not, but isn't that his choice to make?"

"No."

"No?" The resentment in her tone lessens as she realises nothing she can say will change my mind. "You're going to lose him."

"You can't lose something you never really had."

"But Sasha, you've always had him."

The music blares from inside the house, and I feel someone close behind me. Standing on the back porch, wide eyes from my friends settle on me as an arm curves around my waist. Praying it's the one person I want it to be, I turn around, only to experience full-blown disappointment. "Jay?"

Jay is the bad boy from the shitty part of town that every girl wants to fix. Older than us, he's rough around the edges, foul-mouthed, and arrogant. There should be no appeal, yet he can't walk in a room without turning heads.

All the girls want him, and all the boys hate him.

"I've been hoping to bump into you." His eyes dart around the room before landing back on mine. "Your sidekicks around?"

Everybody who's anybody knows Jagger, Drix, and Jay hate each other. Nobody can tell you how it started, but the older we all get, the more non-negotiable their rivalry became.

"Yeah, I think they're getting drinks in the kitchen," I lie. "I should go check on them."

I knew better than to be seen talking to him. I was already on shaky grounds with both Drix and Jagger, and this would just send us tumbling into overdrive.

"Has anyone told you, you're a really bad liar? I know they're not here."

"Fine, they're not here," I huff. "What do you want?"

"I thought we could hang out."

"Nope." I shake my head, and step back, farther away from him. "Whatever game you're playing, I'm not in."

"Are you sure?" He leans in, his mouth just beside my ear. "I think I've got some information that will change your mind."

A shiver runs through me, the sneakiness in his voice, a warning I should walk away.

"Word on the street is Drix has been busy sticking it to Bethany."

Don't believe him, Sasha, he's lying.

Drix and I hadn't spoken in weeks. The deadline for me to show up at his house and say I made a mistake came and went. Instead, I lay holed up in my room for the rest of that weekend, crying more tears than I thought I had.

I don't know what I expected, but I didn't expect him to disappear into thin air. Isolating himself from everyone, he shows up for the important stuff. School. Sports. Jagger. Anything that might mean he'll bump into me is a no-go zone.

"Why would I believe you?" I challenge.

"I got eyes and ears everywhere around here, pretty girl."

I broke up with him for this reason. To allow him to be with someone who would be for him what I couldn't. Maybe Jay is right. Maybe Bethany is it.

"So, I'll ask you one more time, you in or out?"

"I don't know what you're expecting from me, but we can only hang as friends."

While a little voice in my head knew better and was screaming at me to walk away from Jay and his schemes, there was another voice. The voice that reminded me I pushed Drix away, Jagger was having a hard time looking at me, and Bethany was obviously waiting in the shadows for her moment to shine. A new friend wasn't such a bad idea, even if it was Jay.

It could be a twisted version of a fresh start. I didn't care what Jay thought of me, with him I wouldn't need to play nice with Bethany, or hide my hurt from losing Jagger, as well as Drix. With him, the circle of people would be different. Everyone wouldn't know about me and Drix and ask if I was okay. If I let myself, I could use Jay, as much as I know he's using me, and just let it all go.

"No worries, pretty girl. I'll take what I can get."

"He hasn't been mine for way longer than he ever was." The memory brings about nostalgia that I often try to avoid. But every now and then talking about it makes it real, and I need that. So much time has passed I often wonder if I've made up how much I love him, or how much I hurt him.

"That's bullshit," Emerson argues. Her passion is admirable. It's how I know Jagger didn't ever stand a chance against her. "All that is, is labels. He's been there and loved you through it all."

"You think, I think he hasn't done enough?" Uncertain I'm understanding her, I clarify. "You think that's why we're not together?"

"I'm just trying to piece it all together."

"It's not that complicated." I look out onto the field, turning my body away from hers. "I'm sorry if that disappoints anyone, but it all comes down to one simple truth." My voice cracks at the one thought that plagues me. "He's perfect. I'm not."

Thinking the conversation is over, I'm surprised when she grabs my hand. "I'm not going to make a deal about the last thing you said, because I know it hurts. But it's not true." She gives my hand a firm squeeze. "Everybody is perfect in their own way."

Clearing her throat, she places her hand back in her lap, and I rub my nose to hold back the tears. "So, what happened with Jay?"

A soft laugh leaves my mouth. "Much to my surprise he actually grew on me. We spent a few months hanging out, and I guess you could say I kinda liked him."

Drix and Jagger's loud screams have me doing a quick scan of the field, making sure Dakota isn't hurt. Realising they're just mad about a hand ball, I look back at Em. "It wasn't like what I felt with Hendrix. Nothing was ever like that, but it was fun. Carefree."

"Past all the bullshit, I opened up to him, and he got me through a really hard time. I knew he could be a prick of a kid, but behind closed doors he let himself be young and funny. The facade faded."

"Sounds like he made you happy."

"He filled a gap for a while," I say, wistfully, remembering the brief amount of happiness I felt with him before it went to shit. "But I stupidly gave him my virginity and he ghosted me."

"What?" Her face blanches "I didn't see that coming."

"The ghosting hurt, but what did I expect? He was notorious for treating people like shit, and true colours always come out in the end." I let out an exhausted sigh, the trip down memory lane more than I bargained for this morning. "I found out later Jagger had told him to stay the fuck away from me. So, I guess he figured he'd use me to show Jagger who was boss."

"Can I ask why you had sex with Jay?"

"That's the million dollar question, right?" It was the question I never had a concrete answer for. I remember the headspace I was in at the time, and the reasoning I used to justify it, but now it's just another reason to be mad with myself. It's been my motive for raising a daughter who will never fall victim to the traps of insecurity, and second guesses. "I'd placed such a big deal on sex with Hendrix. I don't even know why, all my friends were doing it. Hell, even my mum thought I was.

"I knew sex changed things, and I was scared of change. We'd already gone from friends to lovers, and I would have a moment of panic every day, worried I'd fuck it up. I managed to do it anyway." The tears from earlier find their way back, and I'm grateful my sunglasses are hiding my pain. "So, I thought what the heck, you're never going to be able to have that special moment with Drix, anyway. I dove right in, knowing nothing would ever compare." I lower my chin to my chest and let the tears flow. I was right in thinking nothing would compare, and I've been paying the price in different types of currencies for as long as I can remember. I take a deep breath, and my breath comes back out in hiccups. "It was childish and stupid, and it didn't take long for me to see that, but by then the wheels were already set in motion." The noise of the game fades, as I look from Jagger and Drix to Dakota. My life's awkward triangle. "I didn't have time to worry about all the mistakes I'd made. I had to make sure none of them touched my newborn baby."

eleven

HENDRIX

"Hey, Drix, you coming for drinks?" Evan, one of my co-workers asks me.

"I don't know, man." I climb into my car to get out of the sun. Leaving the door ajar, I turn the air conditioning on, hoping the release of the heat will be quickly replaced by the stream of new, cool air.

"Come on," Stacey interjects, walking up beside Evan. "When was the last time you came out for drinks? Actually, when was the last time you did anything for fun?"

I think back to last Friday night with Taylah. "Are you saying I'm boring?"

"Yes. That's what she's saying, and she's right." He throws his arm around her casually. "Every week feels worse than the one before. Come out."

"Why does this feel like an intervention?"

Evan shakes his head in protest, while Stacey nods taking it as an invitation to inform me that she's apparently not pleased with how my life is going. "Growing old alone doesn't look good on you."

"What does going out have to do with growing old or being alone?"

"You're always too busy being at everyone's beck and call you never take time for yourself."

Her words sting. The truth usually does. So, I defer and get back to the original conversation starter. "Where are we going?"

"Yay." Stacey claps excitedly. "What if we all go home and change? Dinner first? Make a night of it?"

"Fine with me. Evan?" I tip my head in his direction. It's more of a plea than a question.

"Yeah of course, but, I'm going to bring Kat."

"I'll bring Chris," Stacey adds.

Great. Now I'm fifth wheeling it. "I'm going to get going," I announce. "Text me with the time and place, and I'll see you both later."

Now that it's all set in stone, and Evan and Stacey got their way, we don't bother with goodbyes. The thirty-degree day is enough to hurry us along.

Driving home, Stacey's words play on repeat. They merge with the last two weeks of flirting between Taylah and I. After dinner, she tried avoiding me for a few days. I wish I knew why, but my gut says it was the Sasha reminder. She responds to my texts, but she flat out refuses to see me.

Eventually, the whole putting other people first will end up in me being old and alone. I remember how I felt in Taylah's presence. Light and casual, and I remind myself I have to start chasing what I want. I can't be living in a self-imposed exile from life because I'm standing on the outskirts, too busy waiting for something extraordinary to happen instead of finding it, grabbing it and making it mine.

At the next red light, I grab my phone out of the cup holder beside me and find her number. Without second guessing myself, I tap the screen and call her.

The rings keep going and the adrenaline starts to leave through every available exit. Trying not to focus on what pursuing this means, or the fact that she's hell-bent on ignoring how good dinner together was.

"Pick up. Pick up. Pick up." I check the dashboard clock, maybe she's still working? The naive, untainted part of my brain believes if she answers then I'm on the right track. That there's hope I won't be stuck on this crazy merry-go-round of my past dictating my future, maybe there's still time to change my old and lonely status.

"One second," she answers, but the unexpected greeting throws me off. She comes back, her breathing a little heavier. "Hello?"

"Uh, hey. Taylah, it's m—"

"I know who it is, Sexy, I've been texting this number for two weeks." She clicks her tongue. "I've just been too busy to answer your calls."

"Sassy, as always, I see."

"Don't act like you would want it any other way." I hear her smile, my memory sketching up the way her lips twist to the side whenever she's being mouthy. It makes me want to see her even more.

"Look, I called to see if you wanted to come out with me tonight? I really want to see you again."

"Like a date?"

"Well." I drag out the word, longer than intended, trying to buy time to answer her question. "It's a work thing. A few other people will be there."

"God, Sexy, you sure know how to make a girl feel special."

Silently, I hit the heel of my palm on my forehead, repeatedly, while the awkwardness progressively gets worse. "Come on, Crazy." I use my nickname for her, hoping to salvage the conversation and the outcome of tonight. "I'm trying, aren't I? Which is more than I can say for you. I keep trying to call and you keep trying to avoid me."

"I just had some things I needed to think through," she admits. "Trying to play it cool. Not wanting to seem too eager."

"Taylah," I say her name with a chuckle. "You propositioned me for sex the first time we met."

"Actually, it was the second, and I'm kidding." Her voice becomes softer, the earnest loud and clear. "I was just waiting for the timing to be right."

I don't press her for answers. With Taylah, I know they'll

always come, I just have to respect her timing. "So, you think I can pick you up in an hour?"

"How about I meet you there, and if you're lucky you can drive me home."

"Crazy," I say, irritated. "Let me pick you up."

"You said this wasn't a date," she reminds me.

"No, that's not what I said."

"Well you didn't confirm that it was," she bites back. "So, until I figure out your covert reason for inviting me, this is called compromise. What's it going to be, Sexy?"

I pull up into my driveway, as the possibility of seeing her turns from probable to certain. The last five minutes mightn't have gone as planned, but the outcome sets me at ease, relief coursing through me. "I'll text you the details."

We're about to be seated for dinner and Taylah still hasn't shown. Unless I've read her wrong, she doesn't seem like the type to stand me up, but history makes me cautious either way.

"A table for six, huh?" Stacey has been frothing at the mouth since I told her I invited someone. "Why didn't you pick her up?"

"Can we just hold off on the twenty questions, and see if she shows up."

"Oh, she showed up," Evan interrupts, staring at the doorway.

My eyes follow his line of sight, and there she is walking

toward our table after being given instructions by the waiter. She waltzes in like she owns the place, every single eye trained on her every single move.

The best thing is, she's only looking at me. Her mossy green gaze meets mine, swimming with sex and secrets no man could ignore.

Her black dress is the perfect contradiction. High neck, short sleeves, long enough you can only see her painted toes in her forest green, suede heels. It's modest in all the right places until a perfectly toned leg peeks out of a daringly wide, side split, with every calculated step.

She reaches the table, and I clear my throat to greet her. "You made it."

"Of course."

We lean into one another, my hand tentatively touching her waist, hers landing on my chest. Placing a soft kiss on her cheek, I speak directly into her ear. "You look beautiful."

She pulls back and looks up at me from under her thick lashes, and smiles. "Thank you."

I introduce her to everyone around the table, their wide eyes impossible to ignore.

The week in between downplayed how hypnotic she is. As we take our seats, her vanilla scent wafts around me, and I know it's more than physical. She fills up the room with her presence and being close enough to touch her is like delicious torture. Her dress splits open, the material loosely falls around her thigh, ruching at the top of her leg holds it all together. Her skin shines like it's peppered with small specks of glitter, and all I want to do is run my hands all over her, while she wraps herself all around me.

One at a time, everything that attracts me to her starts to fill me up; heavy like weights, taunting me, scaring me with her ability to bring me to my knees. I'm not ready for her. Not now, and probably not in this lifetime, but what shakes me is how badly I want to be.

I catch Stacey eyeing me from across the table, while Taylah effortlessly inserts herself into their conversations. Curiosity has her wanting to burst out of her skin, and I can't help but shake my head at her antics. I scoot my chair closer to Taylah's and settle my arm across the back of hers. She looks back at me, biting her bottom lip, her face both shocked and pleased with how close we're sitting. Her hand finds my thigh, so I cover it with mine and slide my fingers through hers.

"Who's ready to check out the menu?" Evan calls out.

Picking up the leather-bound pages, she places it on the table in front of us both, and just like that, we're all comfort and contentment. Like we've done this a million times before.

Agreeing on a set menu, the food starts piling on the table within the next twenty minutes. The conversation flows easily and the wine even more so.

"So, what's it like working for Legal Aid?" Evan's girlfriend, Kat, asks Taylah. "As opposed to having your own practice, I mean."

"My dad used to do what you guys do. His focus was youth

homelessness, and he spent the majority of my childhood working at the City Youth Centre in Surry Hills. You guys know the one, right?" We all nod. Anyone in the field knows with the increasing number of young people sleeping on the street every night, it's the biggest and most accommodating youth refuge in Sydney. "Of course it hasn't always been what it is now, but he was there when it opened and worked there 'til the day he died."

"Oh, shit," Kat says, covering her mouth in embarrassment. "I'm sorry, I wouldn't have asked."

"Don't be silly. It's fine." She waves her hand in front of her nonchalantly, while I squeeze the hand on my thigh, offering some kind of condolences. "Growing up, he used to joke I should be a solicitor, because I could talk my way out of anything. So, after he died and the time came, I combined his love for helping people with my smart mouth, and here I am."

My stomach clenches in disappointment, it's foolish to think in a short time I'm going to know anything about her, especially something as personal as her dad dying. But what hits harder is the unfounded jealousy that anyone would know *anything* about her before me.

"That's really nice," Stacey adds, the awkwardness obviously lingering. Picking the perfect time to salvage the rest of the exchange, the waiter begins placing the second round of dishes on the table, allowing the moment to shift to something new.

While the chatter around us picks up, I take the opportunity to lean into her. "Are you okay?" I ask, checking in.

She turns, our faces close, our eyes only for one another. "Yeah. It's not the first time I've had to tell that story."

"I'm sorry about your dad, I didn't know."

"And what would you have done if you did know? Veto all the questions before I answered them."

"Maybe."

"Sweet." She runs her thumb down the side of my face, while her eyes shine with gratitude. "But it's completely unnecessary. I'm big and old enough to take care of myself."

What if I want to take care of you? The errant thought has me hastily pulling back, breaking the moment. Her hand awkwardly falling away. "Does the food taste okay?"

The change in subject does the trick. Personal space regained and an unimpressed look from all three women sitting at our table. I'm clearly winning at life. The four pairs of eyes heighten every reaction, and I begin to regret bringing her. I don't know how to just be with everyone's eyes on us. It doesn't feel like last week. It feels like a show I have to perform for or a test I have to pass, and she deserves better than that.

She slides her hand off my thigh, and I let her. I fucked up. She has no idea what goes through my head all the time, and with the constant whiplash I manage to give myself, neither do I. I'm all over the place. It's all on me, and she needs to know that, but unfortunately, this isn't the time or place for that.

The rest of the meal is sat in an awkward silence between us, and an excessive, obvious attempt of inclusion from everyone else.

The pretence is hard to keep up with, and I find myself counting down the minutes till we can get out of here, and maybe I can make it right.

"I'm just going to the bathroom," she announces. And it takes no less than ten seconds for all eyes to turn on me.

"What the fuck was that?" Stacey asks.

"Just let it go, Stace."

"One minute you two are close enough to kiss and then the next you act like she's got some fucking contagious disease. She's really nice—"

"And fucking hot," Evan adds.

"Really? With your girlfriend right there," I say, pointing at Kat.

"What, she doesn't care. Do you, honey?" She smiles and shakes her head, just as he kisses her cheek. "It's the truth. She's the complete package and you're going to fuck it up."

"Thanks for the vote of confidence, you guys."

Having a little too much to drink, they're the king and queens of opinions. Thinking they know best for me and Taylah.

"Listen." Stacey gets up out of her seat with a slight sway, the alcohol clearly making an appearance. "Kat and I are going to go to the bathroom, you guys go next door to the bar, and we'll meet you there."

"I don't know, guys. I should go after her, or just take her home."

"Take her home," she scoffs. Like an older sister, Stacey narrows her eyes at me and lays down the law. "Let me work my magic, because right now, there's no way she's getting in a car with you."

twelve

TAYLAH

I'm washing my hands when the door swings open and a tipsy Kat and Stacey walk in. I quickly cover up my surprise with a smile. "Going to the bathroom?" I ask casually, choosing not to ask them directly if they came in here to check up on me.

They flank me from either side, pretending to use the other free basins in the bathroom. "We just wanted to freshen up before we go to the bar," Stacey says while taking her lipstick out of her clutch. She eyes me through the mirror, as she meticulously applies each pale pink layer.

"Oh, I don't think I'm going to come to the bar." I break eye contact and move over to dry my hands. "Dinner was beautiful, though. Thanks for letting me crash."

"You didn't crash," Kat corrects me. "You were invited."

I smile in response, because I really don't want to have whatever conversation this is. I don't know these women, and while they're lovely, Hendrix and I aren't even a thing, let alone anybody else's business.

Facing the mirror again, I look at both of them. "I appreciate whatever this is, but I really just want to go home."

"He didn't mean it," Stacey blurts out.

"I don't want to be rude, because you guys have been nothing but nice to me, but I don't want to have this conversation with anyone else but Drix. And even that might be a bit of a stretch considering how I'm feeling right now."

"I know the alcohol is going to my head, but I'm not drunk enough to not notice he likes you. An—"

"Stacey, let's give her a moment, and wait for her outside," Kat warns.

"Fine, but can you just promise to hear him out."

"Sure."

They walk out, and as usual, whenever I'm with or think about Hendrix, I'm left feeling like another piece of the puzzle is missing. He doesn't give much away, and it seems like everything, and anything can change for him in a split second.

If I just go home, I can think about whether this is really worth anything. Leaving dinner last week, I was reminded again that Sasha is a big part of his life, if nothing more than because she's Dakota's mother. It seems too soon to ask if I'm ready for that, yet I can't work out why I want more from him. My body might want me to be underneath his a time or two, but something in my gut has me worried all decisions up to this point are fuelled by Sasha. As if he feels compelled to prove she doesn't have a hold on him.

I may be sporadic and carefree, but I'm not stupid, and If I can avoid getting hurt, I want to try that option first.

When we text, I'm content with just sex, but talking about work last week, and sitting with his friends now, I'm getting a glimpse into his world, away from Jagger and Emerson. But even if it feels like something more, I won't be someone's fill-in girl.

I check my reflection one more time before facing the firing squad outside. Stacey is right. I just need to talk to him. He needs to be honest, and tell me what it is he wants. If he wanted sex, he would've already gotten it, but there's something between us. I don't know what it is, but it's there, desperate to take hold and flourish, and I can't walk away from that. Even if I know he's going to break my heart in the process.

Relief hits me when I walk out, and nobody is waiting for me. Straightening my back, I wear my usual confidence and meet them all back at the table. Except only Hendrix is there. With his head in his hands, it's hard not to feel for the grown man who looks so helpless, sitting alone in a full restaurant.

"Drix." He looks up at me, and I can't read him at all. I want to grab his hand, take him next door and load him with some alcohol so he can relax, but I know better. I can't excuse his behaviour, because my empathy for him far outweighs my hurt feelings. "You okay if I go home?"

He stands and walks around the table. The distance between us is reserved, unsure if he's welcome any closer. "Can I take you?"

"I'd rather you didn't. We can just call it a night, forget this ever happened and think long and hard about whether we should repeat it."

"It wasn't that bad, was it?" he asks, clearly taken aback.

"Drix. I like you. I don't know what that means yet, but I'm okay if you don't reciprocate those feelings."

"I didn't say that," he argues defensively.

"Just let me finish. Maybe you're just not ready because of whatever it is you've got hidden in your past." I hold my posture, determined to get the words out. "But you're going to need to find someone else to be your practice girlfriend."

"Practice girlfriend?"

"I don't want to get shut down every time your thoughts go back to her."

He jerks his head back, my admission shocking him. "This isn't about her."

"Well." I raise my eyebrow sceptically. "When you're ready, you can tell me what it's about."

He holds his hand out as an invitation. "Come with me next door."

Hesitantly I take him up on the offer and slip my hand in his. "Stacey is really invested," I say as we get closer to the bar. "You do know I can't be friends with her though, right?"

"What? Why?"

"Her and Jagger had a thing."

He looks at me, puzzled. "You know about that?"

"Of course."

"I'd hardly call it a thing, and it was before he met Emerson, anyway." It's cute how he's defending Jagger, and if it were anybody else but my best friend I would agree completely with his train of thought.

"I know, but Emerson isn't a fan. And if she isn't a fan—"

"Then you're not either," he finishes for me. He gives me his sweetest smile. "You think you can make an exception for me tonight?"

"Considering she checked on me in the bathroom, I think I can let it slide for now. "

We reach the door, and he looks at me just before he pulls it open. Vulnerable, his eyes slowly let their guard down. "Thank you for staying."

"Don't make me regret it, okay?"

Excited when we walked in hand in hand, his friends made sure to never leave us alone, chatting and offering us drinks every chance they get; making it impossible for Drix and I to discuss anything from earlier.

If they weren't so nice, I'd be irritated, but only a bitch would be mad at people trying to make her feel welcome and comfortable.

Not wanting to drink too much, just in case we do end up speaking later, I take small sips of wine, in between huge glasses of water. Hendrix sits close, closer than in the restaurant, and close enough to touch me. Whether it's his arm around my shoulders, or his hand grazing my thigh, a weight has been lifted, and the difference is unmissable.

I'm not one for games. It requires energy I don't have, so instead of keeping him at a distance, I revel in the simplicity of his company. Every touch is like a white flag, and every time I willingly surrender.

Conversation is light, everyone glad to unwind, and escape the weekly grind. I learn Stacey and Chris got together a little after Jagger and Emerson, and they'll be moving in together soon. I find out Evan is going to propose to Kat, he's just waiting for the right moment. And my favourite part is hearing them talk about Hendrix. Whether they're all giving each other shit, or they're telling me how great he is, I realise I'm in the presence of someone who might just be worth the heartache.

As the night progresses, the lights in the bar get darker, and the music gets louder. Changing from the after-dinner crowd to the all-nighter crowd, I decide I'm ready to go home. Not wanting to interrupt Hendrix's conversation with Chris and Evan, I dig my phone out of my bag and text him.

Me: *You ready to drive me home?*

From the corner of my eye, I wait for him to see the text. He doesn't even look up at me, while he types back, and the charade makes me giddy.

Hendrix: *I've been ready since you strutted in with that side split showing off your gorgeous legs.*

I can't help but smile, remembering exactly how I felt as I walked toward the table with his gaze penetrating through me.

Me: *Come on, Sexy. Let's go before I change my mind.*

"You little minx." Stacey flicks my exposed knee, immediately getting my attention. "Were you just sexting, Drix?"

Grinning like a fool, I shake my head. "No, I just asked if he was ready to go."

"To go, and have sex, you mean."

"Who's having sex?" He towers over us, his eyes dancing with desire as he directs the question to me.

"Not us," I say, shocking only Kat and Stacey.

Drix, just laughs, and tips his head toward the exit. "Ready?"

I do the rounds, with Hendrix's hand on the small of my back. Together we say goodbye and they all tell me how happy they are Drix and I came out, and how they hope we'll all do it again some time. It doesn't go unnoticed that it seems to be the first time in a long time Drix has been out with his work friends, or how happy it's made them. I add it to my list of things we can talk about.

Once and for all, I'm decidedly determined to solve the mystery that is Hendrix Michaels.

We get to the car and I groan at the thought of having to lift myself up to get in. "Seriously, Drix. If I'm going to ever dress up to go somewhere with you again, we're taking my car."

He comes up beside me and opens the door. Pressing himself up behind me, one hand latches onto my waist, the other holds my hand. Allowing him to help me with my balance, smoothly I raise one leg and lift myself up. His hand glides down the curve of my hip, resting right under my arse as he pushes me the rest of the way.

Casually I settle in the seat, as he watches me with a smug look across his face. "If we take your car, then I can't do that." He winks. "And I really like doing that."

He closes the door, and I roll my eyes at him, as he walks around the front of the car. When he gets in, he's still smirking, proud of his efforts.

"Where's your phone?" he asks as the car wakes up, rumbling beneath us.

"In my bag."

"Sync it up." He presses the screen a few times, and the words 'Connect to Taylah's iPhone' flash on the screen.

"What's that about?" I point to my name in front of us.

"What?" He shrugs. "I like it when you sing for me."

Turning my head, I look out the window, hiding my flushed

face. "You know I'm not actually singing *for* you, right?"

"For my sake, let's pretend, okay?"

Reaching for my phone, I connect it to the car stereo and look for a song. "And, you don't care what I pick?"

"Nope," he says, letting the end of the word pop. "Sometimes surprises are good."

Shawn Mendes's voice surrounds us both, singing about being nervous, self-conscious and little too excited. Alternating between humming and singing, I lose myself in the song, lip syncing along to the lyrics. Feeling more relaxed and a little less tongue tied as each moment passes, I watch the streets pass me by waiting to see which one of us breaks the ice first.

I catch him glancing at me from the corner of his eye, as the song comes to an end. Instead of the intermittent silence I'm expecting, Shawn's voice starts up again.

I look at him wanting an explanation, but he ignores my questioning, giving me instructions instead. "Sing it again for me, Crazy."

After listening to the song no less than fifteen times, we arrive in front of my house. The music stops, and my stomach churns with anxiety.

On the surface, he and I know how to be. We can smile and flirt, exchange touches and share glances, but now it's only us;

bare, and exposed, and I'm not sure if I'm ready to hear his truth.

Rummaging through my purse, I pull out my house keys and take hold of the door handle. "I don't really know where to go from here," I confess.

"I hate that I made you nervous around me." I don't rush to ease his conscience choosing to see where he takes the conversation instead. "I envisioned such a different outcome for tonight when I called you, and now I just feel like shit for fucking it up."

"It's okay to change your mind and decide you made a mistake by asking me out."

"God, Crazy, you're not a fucking mistake." A pained expression flashes across his face and I don't know if I've hurt him, or he's hurt for me. "Tonight just caught me off guard."

"Drix, I'm just as understanding as the next person, but I don't want you to feel like you owe me." Doubtful, I push him, giving him the out he needs, even if I so desperately don't want him to take the bait. "You obviously have stuff going on, and I'd rather call it a day, than have you convince yourself to enjoy my company." I place my hand on his knee in comfort. "We can live the rest of our lives bumping into one another at Jagger and Emerson's place, it's no big deal."

"And what? Wonder what it would've been like every time I look at you?"

"Maybe that's just how it's meant to be between you and me."

He shakes his head vehemently. "It doesn't feel right to end it before we've even given it a try."

"Drix, we barely know each other."

He turns his head, his eyes studying mine while he asks me what seems to be a random question. "Do you know how many women I've given my number to?"

"No," I answer. "I also don't really know what that has to do with anything."

"The answer is none." He pushes strands of my hair behind my ears, like he needs to take a better look at me. "I'm a fuck and run type of guy. It doesn't paint me in the best light, but it's the truth. I'm the one that will take the number if I want it, and call if I need it." Surprised, my face pulls back ever so slightly, but enough for him to notice. His fingers move from behind my ears, down the side of my face, until he's holding my chin. My attention is all on him. "And while ripping that dress off you has been high on my list of things to do since I first laid eyes on you tonight. I think you should know." He pauses, dramatically, leaning over until his lips hover over mine. The air between us becomes thick and tight, the idea of kissing becomes a deep rooted need that sends tingles through my body in anticipation. "Crazy," he rasps, bringing me back to the moment. "This is the first time I don't want to fuck and run."

His admission opens the floodgates, restraint and sensibility disappearing, only to be replaced by the reality of his confession. What it means for me, what it means for him, and what it means for us right now.

Lips find mine, and for a split second time stands still for the two people who shouldn't make sense. Unmoving, we hold onto one another, hands on either side of our faces. We start a slow, yet passionate exploration, tongues that meet in greeting. *Hello. I'm here. I want you.*

Gentle turns to needy, and suddenly I'm drowning in the simplest form of pleasures. His tongue strokes the inside of my mouth, leaving marks on my memory, and impressions on my heart. I return everything he gives me with a fervour I didn't know I possessed, submitting to our complicated honesty, imperfect truths, and everything that makes this moment real.

Reluctantly we pull apart, and he leans his forehead into mine.

"Do you want to come inside?" I ask breathlessly.

He drops one last chaste kiss before opening the door, and hopping out. Wordlessly he accepts my invitation.

thirteen

HENDRIX

The second the door closes, I refrain from pushing her up against the wall and finishing what we left off in the car. My mind knows taking it slow is the right thing to do, but with her, I feel like my wings are no longer clipped, and I want to take her, and fucking fly.

She stares at me with her tousled hair, bruised lips, and bright eyes, and I wonder how the fuck I'm ever going to keep my hands off her.

"Are we just going to stand here staring at one another?" she teases.

"It's either that or I'm going to strip you naked, and fuck you." I sink my hands into the front pockets of my jeans, needing physical restraints.

"That sounds promising." She begins to waltz her way to me, chewing on her bottom lip. Her eyes are playful, her body nothing short of temptation.

"Don't get any ideas," I warn, taking more steps backward. "We're taking it slow."

The back of my legs hit the edge of her couch, as she reaches for me, latching on to my shirt collar. She wraps her arms around my neck and moves closer. Pressing her breasts against my chest, she whispers in my ear. "Are you sure?"

My self-control wanes as I run the tip of my nose down the length of her neck. I drop kisses on her exposed skin, losing the ability to form coherent words and thoughts. Too caught up in the fog, that is her.

"What am I going to do with you?" I murmur.

"We both want it, Drix."

Seeking out her lips, she meets me halfway, moaning into my mouth, making my cock harder than I thought possible. I groan and slip my hand through the slit of her dress, gripping her bare arse, wrapping her leg around my waist. "Fuck now, talk later, okay?"

She drops her leg and takes my hand. "Follow me."

Leading me to her room, the intimacy changes. Even though our hands are still tangled, and my dick is still very much hard, the sex has been siphoned out of the air, replaced with adoration and wonder. There's so much more to the room than just four walls. It's sensual and spontaneous, and if there was any way I could forget how privileged I was to be in the presence of this woman, this room was my reminder.

"Did you draw these?" On each wall is a life-size sketch, two are landscapes, but it's the one behind the large king bed that I can't stop looking at. It's the epitome of sadness and beauty. "That's you, isn't it?" I tear myself away from the drawing and face Taylah, whose nervousness has her staring at the wall, and unable to look at me. "I'm sure you already know this, but you're really talented."

"I didn't tell you I drew them."

"You didn't have to."

I pull her to me so her back is pressed against my front, both of us standing at the edge of the bed, staring at the wall. Softly I drape her hair across her shoulder and run my fingers down the curve of her neck. "Tell me about the picture." I take hold of the small black coated zipper and watch the expanse of her back become more visible by the second. The dress loosens, revealing her shoulders, the material needing only a slight tug to fall to the floor and leave her naked.

Kissing her is inevitable, her skin luring my mouth to her shoulders, my tongue drawing invisible lines between her faint freckles.

"Sometimes there's a moment in your life where everything, slowly, yet surely begins to make sense," she starts, her body shivering beneath my touch. "Where the past finally stays where it belongs, and the future is somewhere you actually want to be."

My focus switches from her body to her words and back again. Entranced and intrigued, by both, her body is ethereal, her words are prophetic.

"Are you exactly where you want to be?"

She nods, and I take it as an invitation to tip her dress off the edge and watch it fall down her body. The vulnerability of her statement and the power of her nakedness turns the moment from a passionate frenzy to an emotional seduction.

She steps out of the dress and spins on her heels to face me. "Is this where *you* want to be?"

With almost every inch of her on display and mine for the taking, the challenge is clear. I reach for the back of my shirt, stretching it over my head, and throwing it to the side of the room. "What do you think?"

We launch at one another, skin on skin, and we're back where we started. Cradling her body to me, I rest a knee on the edge of the mattress and let us fall. Our mouths talk, our lips take, our tongues give. Lust turns into desperation as we wrap ourselves up in pleasure.

I endeavour to taste every inch of her skin, moving from her lips to her neck, down to her filled out breasts. Her nipples stand at attention, begging for my tongue. With every taste, my dick gets harder, wanting nothing more than to break free.

My mouth makes its way down to the edge of her panties, smelling her arousal before I see it. Hooking two fingers into her waistband, I rise, slowly, and drag the lace strips of material down her legs. Instinctively, her legs begin to fall together, but I hold her knee in protest. "Leave them open."

They lax as I discard my own layers of clothes, our impatience bubbling at the surface. She looks at me with intoxicating desire. "You're even sexier with no clothes on."

I grip my cock at her appraisal, warding off the impulsive need I have to thrust myself into her, hard and fast.

"What are you waiting for?" she goads, her fingertips teasing the top of her open slit.

Never having to agonise over what I say with Taylah, the words tumble out without thinking twice. "I can't work out which hole I want to stick it in."

She smiles. Full blown. Megawatt. A smile reserved for compliments, not my uncensored fantasies. She gets up on her knees and rests her arms on my shoulders. Instinctively I take hold of her waist. "Answer me this. Is this going to happen more than once?"

I caress her heavy breast. "What do you think?"

"Well then don't think too hard, there'll be time for every hole." She bites my bottom lip. "More than once."

"Fuck, Crazy, you have the filthiest mouth."

"And you don't even know all the things I can do with it." She free falls backward on to the bed, with a teasing smile on her face, and I follow. I kiss the smile off her face, transforming it into a moan as my finger slides through her wet pussy.

My thumb rubs softly over her clit, while a second finger fucks her. The contrast has her arching beneath me, breathless and wanton. Small tremors flitter through her, as her heat cinches around my fingers. "We're only just getting started, Crazy." I add pressure to her throbbing bud, and she bucks up against me. I watch her find euphoria as my fingers hit her perfect spot.

I kiss up her body, capturing her loud moan with my mouth; savouring her moment of bliss in all the ways I can. My shaft nudges at her entrance, the head of my cock, slick and dripping, ready for the final round.

Slipping inside of her is like the light at the end of the tunnel. Warm and waiting, my breath catches in my throat as she sheaths my cock with her pussy. Groaning, I thrust into her, craving the friction.

Our worlds collide in a rush of frenzied, rough, and crazed kisses. Hard and desperate, I drive myself into her, and she arches herself into me. I fall in lust with the way she feels underneath my body and stretching around my cock.

She digs the heels of her feet into my arse, as I pound into her harder. "God, Drix, I'm going to come again."

A strained chuckle leaves my mouth. "That's the idea, babe." I slip my finger between us, rubbing and pinching her clit, wanting to entice her orgasm along.

She clutches herself to me, digging her nails into my back as she reaches her peak. Her breathing becomes more rapid as her body turns from tightly coiled to carefree in a single thrust.

My own release sits heavy in my balls, on the precipice, teasing me every time I feel her clench around my cock. I pound into her with ferocity, challenging myself to tip her over the edge one last time.

I slam into her, hard, fast and deep, the cries of my name from her hoarse throat spurring me on. Everything turns black as I get lost in the primal need to give and take. Heat creeps up my spine, and the final thread holding us together snaps.

Coming down from the high, we kiss one another; unhurried, sated, and full of languid satisfaction.

I let myself deflate against her, floating on air for the first time in a very long time.

"You're really good at that." She smiles while kissing me, and like a transferable tattoo, the shape of my mouth suddenly matches hers.

Rolling off her, I tuck my hands underneath my head. "So, I've been told."

Sitting up, she demurely moves her legs over the side of the bed and looks back at me mischievously. "Maybe I'll just keep you here."

"What? And just use me for my dick?" I ask, conceitedly.

She glances down at my semi-hard cock, licks her lips and innocently shrugs. Stretching across the bed, I snake my arm around her waist and tuck my hand in between her legs. "Will you at least feed me?"

She leans into me, giving me a quick peck on the lips. "As many meals as you want." Untangling herself from me, she stands up and begins rummaging through a pile of clothes sprawled on a reading chair in the corner of her room. "But, I need to feed myself first."

"Dinner wasn't enough for you?" I joke while I also get off

the bed and find my underwear.

"Well." Facing me, she exhales loudly while covering her body, with a geometrically patterned, floor-length satin gown. "I may as well get this out of the way before we go any further." Slumped shoulders, serious expression, I have no idea what's coming next. "I hate set menus," she blurts out. "And I hate everything about sharing food."

Hysterical laughs trip out of my mouth, and a pillow unexpectedly hits me in the head. Picking it up off the floor, I throw it back at her. She dodges it, hands on her hips, biting back her own laughter.

"Is that why you didn't eat much?" She hands me my boxer briefs, throwing my jeans with the rest of her clothes.

"You don't need those unless you plan on going home."

With no intentions of leaving her, her house or her body, I forget about the jeans and continue the discussion about food "I'm going to have to hear more about how painful tonight's set menu was for you."

"Don't even joke, Hendrix. Do you know how hard it is to stop at one duck spring roll? These places. they give you four and there are five people, but you want two. I'm bad at math, but I know it equals me leaving the restaurant hungry."

"You're serious about this."

She narrows her eyes at me. "The question is why aren't you?"

Following her into the kitchen, I cross my arms, and lean back on to the bench. "I've really never given it this much thought."

Opening her pantry, she pulls out a shake and make pancake bottle, along with maple syrup, icing sugar, and a bag of chocolate chips. Placing them on the counter, she looks up at me. "You think I'm crazy, don't you?"

I kiss the tip of her nose. "You didn't get that nickname for nothing."

"So," she says, flittering around the kitchen for additional needs. "Do you want some of my famous choc chip pancakes?"

"I could definitely eat pancakes, do you want help?"

She hands me the plastic bottle. "If you could fill it up with water and shake it using those muscles of yours, I would greatly appreciate it."

Snatching it from her, I fill it up to the designated line. I flex my arm while shaking the bottle. "Is this what you meant?"

"God, how will I ever make pancakes without you."

"You're in for some hard times, Crazy."

Rolling her eyes, she places a silver mixing bowl between us. "Pour it in here."

As I do, she empties the chocolate chips into the bowl also. "You know they have the chocolate chip version of these shake and makes."

"I am aware, but sometimes when I go on a random health binge, I snack on chocolate chips and convince myself it's not breaking the rules because they're so small."

"It's totally breaking the rules."

"Ha. Ha. That's funny." She hands me a whisk. "I don't

remember asking you."

"I'm sorry, did I sign up for kitchen hand?"

"You got to earn your keep around here, that dick will only get you so far."

I click my tongue. "Is that a challenge?"

"You're welcome to prove me wrong *after* I eat the pancakes."

"Deal." Grabbing her shoulders, I nudge her out of the kitchen. "Go, be busy, and these will be ready in no time."

"Drix, I'm kidding I—"

"No," I cut her off. "Let me do it for you."

"Fine, I'll just be taking photos of you in your underwear slaving over the stove."

"Is that necessary?"

"Do you know women at all? This is equivalent to a photo of you with a newborn baby on your chest." She jogs into her room and comes back with her phone in hand. "I'm going to send it to all my friends. Better yet I'm going to post it on Instagram, with the hashtag you wish you were me right now."

Focusing back on the task at hand, I continue making sure the pancake batter isn't lumpy, and adding the chocolate chips. Taylah's explanation of women, babies, and cooking goes straight over my head, as I give her my back and start up her gas stove to cook the pancakes. We're in a comfortable silence, me dead set on the perfect pancakes, and her trying for the perfect picture.

"Do you want to eat on the breakfast bar or the table?"

"You're going to set up too?

"Why not?" I ask rhetorically. "You can get the whole Hendrix Michaels experience."

"Let me do it, it's only fair."

She sets up her cute little four-seat dining table. Two plates, two cups, cutlery, and maple syrup. It's unexpectedly domestic. I pick up the small stainless steel sieve and dust the icing sugar over the stack of pancakes.

Taking myself and the plate to the table, I catch Taylah looking at me with fascination. Being the centre of her attention reminds me of the way I had all her focus when she walked into the restaurant earlier. It's such a heady feeling to have someone look at you, and see something they like. Something they want.

"God, I love breakfast food." She drowns the pancakes with maple syrup, cutting her stack of four into equal quarters.

"You do this often?"

"It's my favourite thing about living on my own."

"Eating pancakes at night?"

"More so eating breakfast food anytime I want." She rises off her seat, ever so slightly, reaching to the middle of the table to pour us both a glass of juice. "Then there's being able to have a television in my room, and being able to eat in said room."

"You had a lot of rules growing up?"

"My mum was such a clean freak. You couldn't even sneeze without her freaking out that something was out of place. As soon as I could afford moving out, I was done." Stopping to take a sip of her juice, she gracefully manages to eat, drink, and talk at the same time. "Don't get me wrong, I know having a clean house and a clean mum is a first world problem, but it's so fucking liberating not to have a woman follow you with a vacuum at all times of the day."

"Makes sense," I say, my mind visualising a younger Taylah feeling irate at her mother's requests. "I remember feeling something similar after moving out of my mum's place."

"Any rules you were happy to break once you left. Something that doesn't make me sound like the only deranged one in the room."

I finish off the pancakes before answering. Stalling. Giving myself a bit of time before taking a visit down memory lane. "My mum didn't care about much, to be honest. She only had two rules. One for Jagger and one for me."

"What were they?" Her voice is cautious as she asks the question, and I wonder if I made it too obvious that I didn't really want to go down this road.

"Jagger's was, don't be like your dad, and mine was…"

"Don't be like your dad," she finishes for me. "What was he like?"

"Absent."

"Safe to say you're a good son then, and didn't break her rules."

"I guess that's one way to look at it." My plate finished, I push it forward and lean back on the chair. "Tell me more rules you broke when you got your own place."

The change in conversation doesn't go unnoticed, but she accepts it anyway. "There's only one more, and it's my personal favourite." Loosening the knot holding her gown together, the swell of her breasts become visible. "No clothes."

My eyes zero in on her tits, while my cock twitches at the possibilities. "How about you explain the no clothes part to me."

Seductively, she licks the syrup off each finger, then opens the rest of her gown. "How about I just show you?"

fourteen

TAYLAH

He's around the table, hands on my body, lips on mine, all before the satin even hits the floor. "You know what else is great about living alone," he murmurs. "We can do this anywhere."

Sucking on my bottom lip, he grips my arse. Lifting me up, he wraps my legs around him and carries me to the nearest kitchen counter. He rests me on the edge, and sticky, maple kisses make their way down my neck. I lean back on my elbows as he bypasses my collarbone, licking each nipple before kissing down the valley of my breasts and beelining for his destination.

The second he reaches the top of my slit, my lungs constrict in anticipation. He changes direction, his mouth teasing me everywhere but where I need him most.

Hands push my thighs farther apart, opening me up, preparing me for him. A swipe of his tongue has me jolting out of my skin, followed by delicious circles around my clit, he becomes the king of teasing, and taunting. He dips his tongue in and out of me; slow and sensual torture.

"You taste like us." Low and gravelly, the sound of his voice against my pussy, and the thought of *us*having a taste sends a rush of hot need through my body and straight to my core.

The tip of his tongue runs back up to my sensitive flesh; biting and licking. The pace picks up, and the burn inside me becomes unbearable. My fingers dig into his scalp, gripping onto his hair as my hips grind against his face. He feasts on me like a starved man, lapping at my dripping centre.

Two fingers sneakily slip inside me, and the intrusion is all I need to feel myself shatter. He sucks my clit through my entire orgasm, the sensation dragging out a long and illicit, "Oh, fuck."

I lay blissfully limp on the counter, unable to talk, unable to move. Rising slowly, the first thing I notice is his wet, smug smile. The second is his dick trying to climb out of his boxers.

I flick my gaze between him and his cock. "Looks like you might need a little help."

He rubs along his length. "Are you offering?"

Sitting up, I open my legs and he steps in between them. I slip one hand into his waistband, the other pushing the material down his legs. Hot and heavy in my hands, I grip his steel-like shaft. A hiss leaves his mouth as I move up and down. "You ready for hole number two?"

"Fuck, Crazy. Stick me somewhere before I blow it like a teenager all over your fucking hands."

Reluctantly I drag my hand out, and push against his chest, leading him to the couch. "Sit."

He puts his hand up, pretending to surrender. "Whatever you say."

Naked, he sinks into the couch, his cock standing tall against his stomach. I drop to my knees, eager to return the favour.

He stares at me. Eyes full of thirst and want. A gaze so potent, I will remember it past this moment.

"Do you even know how fucking exquisite you look right now?"

I lower my head to hide the flush I feel creeping up my face. My heart finds the wrong time to try and claw its way out of my chest, as every single detail of this moment carves out its own space in my memory.

I wrap my fingers around his cock, and it jolts in my hand. A shine of pre-cum coats the tip, and it's the only invitation I need to swipe my tongue through his slit.

His loud groan spurs me on, and with greed, I take him whole, in my mouth. His skin is warm and stretched, the ripple of his veins sliding against my tongue.

Lazily, my head begins to bob up and down his dick while my hands keep busy. One matches my movements, the other tentatively massaging his balls. His hand finds the back of my head and together we gain momentum. We find a rhythm. I suck and stroke. He gets harder and deeper.

"Shit." His voice is strained and desperate like he's on the brink of breaking. "Taylah," he says with urgency. His thrusts become harsher as he hits the back of my throat, his body talking for him, replacing the failed words. I look up at him expectantly, my eyes inviting him to let go. To crash. To fall. To come. Eyes squeezed shut, head tipped back, he empties himself in my mouth. Thick like the tension coursing through his body, it all comes out, filling my mouth and sliding down my throat.

His body sags against the couch, his breathing loud and ragged.

"That good, huh?" I tease.

He leans forward, kissing me, hard and full of purpose. "You got no idea." He stands up, offering me his hand. "Come. Show me your shower."

Both naked, and fulfilled, we wait by the shower stream in contented silence. His front to my back, arms wrapped around my stomach, chin resting on my shoulder. This is different.

In a matter of hours, our time together has shifted. If I thought I wanted to see where things with Drix went before the night took a turn, now I don't know if I'd even be able to walk away.

I could chalk it up to good sex, but I'd be lying. It's him. He's intense. He's addictive. He's all-consuming and the craziest part is he doesn't even know it.

We step into the warm spray, standing face to face. As we stare at one another, words don't feel relevant, and by the way he's lighting me up with his eyes, it's evident he feels it too.

A quick look around has him holding up my loofah and body wash in question. I nod and move farther into the water. I close my eyes wanting to just experience it. Slowly, he draws circles along my skin with the soapy sponge. Leaving suds in his wake, he washes every inch of me with overwhelming reverence.

Raising my arms in the air, I tip my neck back and let the spray cascade all over my hair and body.

"You're so fucking beautiful, you know that?"

I suck in a quick breath, trying to hide how deep his words reach, amazed that this is where we are at right now. Taking the loofah out of his hand, I wash his body. Doing the opposite, I start at his legs, and work my way up, knowing me on my knees in front of him for a second time will drive him wild.

We're back to standing face to face, even closer than minutes before. "You're not too bad yourself."

I switch off the water and pull down the towel that hangs over the glass door. I wrap it around the both of us, bringing him closer. I waste no time, kissing him because I want to, kissing him because right now it's impossible not to.

We kiss until our bodies are dry, and the cold starts to seep in. We kiss out of the bathroom and into the bed, stopping for the small things that lead us to our destination.

I wrap myself around his body, head on his chest, arm over his torso. "Is this weird?" he asks, running his fingers through my hair.

I pretend to not know what he's asking. "What's weird?"

"I can't stop touching you."

Letting my vulnerability seep through, I ask, "Is that bad?

"This whole night has been unexpected, that's all."

I leave the admission alone. It's not like I don't agree, but I don't want to hear doubt, or anxiety if the conversation persists. I would rather listen to my body, feel it through every kiss. Know within myself that this is a deviation from the norm, but it's a good one.

It's an unapologetic attraction where any walls between us become walls around us, keeping everything else out. Every time we touch or kiss, it's like we're abandoning the rest of the world, giving in to our most basic and carnal needs; letting our physical connection bleed into our emotional one.

"Tell me about your drawing."

"When I was nineteen, I planned the trip of a lifetime." With our skin so close, and his heartbeat in my ear, I share my most painful story. "I don't have any siblings, and growing up, as sad as it may sound, my parents, especially my dad, were my best friends. They supported and encouraged me through everything.

"At this stage, I'd finished six months of University. I didn't hate it, but I felt restricted. So, I said to my parents, 'I'm going to hit the pause button, go travelling and come back to finish.'" The stroking of my hair continues, soothing me more than he probably realises. "As usual, there were no complaints or concerns, as long as I came up with the money for my trip myself. I worked my ass off, day and night, to come up with the money, but eventually, I had a perfect amount to know it was happening."

"Where did you work?" he asks, interrupting with unexpected

curiosity.

"I worked in hospitality. Swapped from front of house to bartending; I was a real jack of all trades, depending on what time of the day it was, and I was happy to do it, just to save more money. Plus it was a global industry. If I needed extra cash overseas, it would be easier for me to find a job anywhere, and keep it.

"Anyway, long story short, I saved for the trip, and me and my dad planned it together. Every flight, every trek, every hotel, there was nothing we hadn't thought out. It was his holiday just as much as mine. Him and my mum had done a lot of travelling before they had me, and he was so excited I was going to be able to experience the same things as him."

I close my eyes and count to five, mentally preparing myself for the next part of the story. "Five days before my trip, he dies. Heart attack." My vision blurs as the tears begin to form. The time that's passed seems so insignificant when I talk about the day he died. The ache and the shock always hit me as hard as they did the exact moment I found out. The tears start to fall, and I shift my hand to wipe them, but he stops me. His hand covers mine, keeping them both on his chest.

"Keep going." His invitation to let my guard down opens the floodgates. A small pool of water now forming on his bare skin.

"He was the healthiest person I knew, not one single vice. And in a second he was gone." He threads his fingers through mine, squeezing tightly. Empathy and sympathy evident in his actions. "I wanted to cancel my trip and my mum insisted it wasn't necessary."

"It was probably the grief laced with truth, and our biggest fight to date, but my mum rushed the funeral and had his body cremated in no time. Pushing me to go. She gave me ashes in an urn and told me to lay him to rest around the world, so there was never a corner of the earth that couldn't feel him." More tears fall, as I dredge up the hurt. "I wanted to be there for her, and she said she needed to be alone because she didn't want to rush, and needed to be alone to say goodbye to the love of her life. Her words successfully pushed me onto that plane, and my holiday became a heavy-hearted escape."

A surprise kiss to the top of my head gives me the strength to get through my next sentence. "I cried more tears than I ever thought possible as I left a piece of him and my childhood in every place I visited. It will always be the hardest thing I ever had to do."

"For the sake of the story I have to admit to you I am a huge Phil Collins fan, and my favourite Disney movie is Tarzan, because the whole soundtrack was sung by him." His chest rumbles in soft laughter underneath me, and a small giggle leaves my mouth in following. "When I was younger, my dad had this cassette tape of Phil Collins live, and I listened to it 'til it literally fell apart. The Christmas before he died, I bought him Phil Collins Live in Berlin on DVD, hoping to replace the one I broke.

"So, on my trip, I made a friend." I feel him tense, and I smile to myself, secretly. "For me, it was puppy love at its finest. I followed him everywhere as he became my crutch in all the ways he shouldn't. It was our last night together and I was in my room crying. Overwhelmed by the loss of my dad, my emotions just transferred. Shifting to me being unexplainably upset at leaving Dylan. Next thing you know, I've got a random playlist on, music blaring through my room, and I'm sitting on the balcony of my hotel and ugly crying, oblivious to the world."

Lifting myself off of Hendrix's chest I sit up, pulling the sheets up enough to cover me, and face the reason behind this whole conversation. He watches me as I focus on the drawing, getting lost in my own story.

"As I was crying, 'You'll be in my Heart' by Phil Collins comes on. It was so cheesy and tragic, but it was so perfect. To say I was a mess would be an understatement, in that moment I lost myself to the hurt, but I also let go of it. I hear something from inside the room, and I turn to see Dylan standing there taking pictures."

I look back at Hendrix. Transfixed by my confessions, his eyes don't waver from my face. His attention on me, afraid to miss a thing.

"That moment was a turning point for me," I continue. "Like the universe sent me a message from my dad in song lyrics and I needed to dust off my knees, get up, and keep living. Months after I returned home Dylan sent me the photo in the mail; he'd written the words *The Next Chapter* on the back."

Crawling over to my bedside table, I pull out the original and hand it to Drix. "It became the reminder I needed as I lived my life, and more and more years passed without my dad."

"I moved into this place after I got my first full-time job, it was my next chapter. I sketched the photo on the wall while drinking a whole bottle of wine and listening to Phil Collins on repeat. For days and months after, I added the details to the drawing whenever life got a little bit too much."

I glance over, and he's still staring at the photo. My mind wondering what he sees when he sees it.

"The obvious point of this story is my dad is always with me, but it's the message within the message that resonates more, the older I get—" I cut myself off waiting to see if he looks back at me. He does expectantly like he's waiting on bated breath for my wisdom.

"It's not that inspiring," I warn.

He nudges my knee with the back of his hand. "I want to hear it anyway."

"Whatever it is, I'm going to survive, just like I did the last time. Days, months, years. The time frame doesn't matter. In the end, I want to be able to look back and say, 'I survived it.'"

Lowering my chin to my chest, I simultaneously try and pull the blankets higher up my body, feeling heavily unguarded.

Fingers tip my face up, bringing my eyes to his. "I know it was a while ago, and I said it before, but I really am sorry about your dad."

I nod, accepting his condolences.

He sits up at a ninety-degree angle like he needs a better look at me. He tucks my hair behind my ear before skating his thumb across my bottom lip. "For what it's worth, I'm sure your dad would be so proud of you right now."

He places the softest kiss on my lips, and naturally my body lights up at his touch, ready to take it further. "Stop," he says, moving back. "I owe you an explanation."

fifteen

HENDRIX

The words surprise us both, me more than her. I've never wanted to talk about anything to anyone. Not about my mother, about what went down with Jagger and obviously, not Sasha. Originally I kept things to myself because I didn't want to burden others, but then my burdens turned into secrets, and those secrets have taken charge of my life.

Taylah agreed to me coming over because we had the intention to talk. We may have allowed ourselves to get side-tracked, but she deserves an explanation about tonight, and even if it feels out of character, it's still something I know I can do.

"What are you talking about?" she asks, perplexed.

"Tonight at the restaurant. When it all went to shit. I want to—"

"Drix." She leans forward, stopping short of my mouth.

"We've come so far from that moment."

"I know, but it's the right thing to do."

"Fine." She pulls back, her eyes like laser beams, piercing through me. "What is it that's got you so worked up?""

A few long seconds pass and the ability to speak seems to have gone missing. The rush of confidence, dwindling. I know I can bail, redirect the conversation to anything else and she'll let me.

As stupid as it sounds, I don't know how to talk about myself. I don't share feelings, I don't let anyone in, and I sure as hell don't ever get deep and meaningful with someone I'm sleeping with.

I'm scared of the vulnerability, scared to say something stupid, or even worse, something I can't take back. But the voice inside my head is nagging at me to talk to her, to tell her things. To show her me. "Fuck." Pinching the bridge of my nose, I shake my head like the motion might just make everything make sense.

"God, Drix you're killing me here." She looks around the room, and then back at me. "Lie down."

"What?"

"Lie down. Let's sit the way we were before, and you don't have to look at me."

"But I like looking at you."

"When you're about to fuck me, yeah, but whatever it is you're trying to say has you looking like a fish out of water."

She fusses around with the bedding like she's tucking in a child. I let her. Laying back down, we come together like magnets, her body wrapped around mine, my hands on her, and her head listening to the erratic beats of my heart.

With her dainty fingers roaming around my chest, I stare at the ceiling and let her soothe me into solace. Without admitting to the comfort of not having Taylah's eyes on me right now, I dive straight into the pool of me and her. "This feels a lot more serious than I'm used to," I start. "At the restaurant, I was a dickhead." I feel her trying to get up in protest, so I hold her tighter. "You walked in that restaurant tonight, and sat with me and my friends like you belonged in my life." She stills in my arms like she's waiting for the other shoe to drop. "The reason I turned into a jerk was because I was shocked by how much I wanted you there. You mentioned your dad passing, and the first thing that came to my mind was, 'why don't I know that about her already.'"

"Drix."

"I know it was impossible, but in that split second, I realised I wanted to know things about you. Things everyone knows, things nobody knows.... It shocked me." She sits up and the sheets fall off her back. Naked, wet eyelashes, and red cheeks, she's raw, and on display. The woman in front of me is changing me, and for the first time, I welcome it.

"I don't know what to say when you tell me things like that." Twisting her body, she throws her legs off the edge of the bed. She walks out of the room, giving me a view of heaven, only to come back covering it up.

Even though I'm momentarily distracted by the fact her skin is no longer on display, getting to the bottom of why she stormed out is more important. "What is it?"

"I wasn't going to call you, you know?" She stands in the middle of the room, the distance between us bothering me. "Actually, I was even more surprised you called me."

"But that doesn't explain why you're no longer naked, and standing so far away from me."

"You know why I didn't contact you, right?" she asks, completely bypassing what I just said. The shitty thing is I do. And instead of addressing the elephant in the room, I nod and keep silent, avoiding the conversation I know needs to be had. "It's the same reason I'm so surprised to hear you say you're into whatever this is too."

"Can you come back to bed, please?." She takes a few hesitant steps toward me. "Naked."

The minute she's within reach, I take her hand and pull her on top of me. My head lands on her range of pillows, and my hands hold on to her waist. "I want to see what this is with you. Can that please be enough for now?"

With a heavy resigned breath, she rolls off me, landing on her back, beside me. "I'm not trying to bust your balls, Drix. I'm just trying to make sure I don't get hurt. They're two very different things."

Everything she's saying makes sense, and every essence of my being knows she has every right to feel the way she does. But I'm always the one to think too hard and take too long. Right now, I don't want to be that guy. I just want to feast in this feeling with her for as long as she'll let me.

I don't care if it's too soon, or I don't really know her, or it might just be the really good sex. None of those rules or expectations matter, because with her I enjoy the moment, without worrying about the consequences. With her, my mind is so fucking silent, and that's something I've spent too much time searching for.

"Crazy."

"Yeah."

"I don't want either of us to get hurt."

Turning on her side, she leans on her elbow and rests her cheek on the inside of her hand. "That's good enough for me."

I mirror her pose. "Can you come a little bit closer."

"What do you mean? I'm right next to you."

"But you could be on top of me."

"Oh," she says, pretending to play along. "My bad." She manoeuvres her leg over, straddling me. "This better?"

Kicking the blankets to the side, I grip onto her waist and pull her farther down, her pussy hovering directly above my cock. "We're getting there."

My fingers slide through her folds. Like the gift that keeps on giving, she's wet and wanting. Bringing my thumb to her clit, I begin to rub in a slow, circular motion. She draws in a harsh breath at the contact, and my dick throbs from the power I have over her.

Lowering herself completely, she rubs herself up and down my shaft. My movements become faster, as she drips all over my cock.

"I need you inside me, Drix." She wraps her hands around my

hard, and slick cock, lifting her body up off me. "Please."

"I'm all yours." She slides herself down my dick, and I piston my hips, wanting to feel myself deep-seated inside her. With her eyes on mine, and her lips parted, she looks down at me with nothing but want written all over her face. "Ride me, Crazy."

I splay my hands across her arse, gripping her cheeks through every delicious bounce. Hard and fast, I fuck her and she uses me, both of us racing to the finish line. Close to the edge, I get lost in the vision before me. With golden locks cascading around her shoulders, and dusty rose nipples begging to be sucked, she looks like the angel of seduction, here to bring me to my knees.

Gripping the back of her neck, I pull her face toward me and fuck her mouth with my tongue. Thrusting into her, I'm a man unhinged, ready to explode. My hand finds her swollen clit, and I prepare her to meet me at the edge.

With a final slam down on my cock, her pussy starts to throb around me. Roaring in relief, we ride out the wave; bodies weakening, hearts pounding. High on the rush of being so close to her, all the tension gone, dissolving into nothing.

Her clammy body crumples on to mine, her head nestled perfectly in my neck. "I'm sorry, I don't even have the energy to roll off you." She yawns as I stretch my hand out to throw the blankets over us. "Do you mind if I just lie here for a little?"

Cocooned away from the world, my fingers skate up and down her spine. At peace. Fulfilled. Happy. "You can lay here for as long as you like."

"I can cancel my plans," she yells from the bedroom. "Emerson won't mind."

The morning starts off slow and sluggish, sex and a shower together making it harder for us to part.

"You guys have plans," I call back, as I clean up last night's mess in the kitchen. "I'm not going to fuck that up."

"What about if Jagger comes and the four of us can do something?" With her head tipped to the side, she walks toward me, dressed and glowing, while attaching her earring to her ear.

"Just tell her to bring Jagger, but don't tell her I'm here." A guilty look crosses her face. "Okay, what are the chances she hasn't already told him yet."

"Why? What's the big deal."

"I just want to surprise my brother." It's a half lie. I'm really hoping to avoid giving him time to think of a million questions and reasons of why being here with Taylah is a bad idea. After the way he acted at football practice the other week, having to explain myself to him, is not how I want this to go down.

"So, he doesn't know about us at all? Even the texting?"

"He knows I gave you my number."

"Oh." She nods, slowly meeting me on the same page.

"I told you, I fuck and run. Jagger knows my deal."

"Well, you did the first part right."

"That I did, didn't I?" Finishing up in the kitchen, I make

my way to the couch, and unceremoniously collapse on it. I tip my chin up at her, smugly. "I gave you some good dick, right? Fucked you good and proper."

She stands in front of me, mildly unimpressed. Her earrings secured and her hands on her hips. "I'm sure Jagger would love to hear all about it."

"I've got other things to tell him too, don't you worry."

"You do?"

Leaning over, I grab her, guiding her to stand in between my legs. "I could tell him how we plan to do it all over again tonight." She bites her bottom lip, refusing to smile at my antics. Instead of continuing with the sex talk, I try a little bit of truth. "The most important thing he needs to know is this is undoubtedly one of the best weekends I've ever had."

"Really?" Her voice perks up at my revelation, while a slight flush creeps up to her cheeks. I fold my hands over hers and bring them up to my lips.

"You know it."

Loud knocking cracks through the noise coming from the television. In a few steps, Taylah opens the door and an excited Emerson walks in with an extremely perplexed Jagger behind her. Em's eyes beeline for me, and I can't help but smile at how happy she is to see me.

Every time I see her, I thank the universe Jagger found her. She brought him back to life in a way I don't think Dakota or I ever could.

I stand to hug and greet her when Jagger notices me. His face morphing from mild rage to understanding. He doesn't miss a beat when it comes to any other guy looking or touching his woman. "Relax, it's me, you fucking caveman. No one's trying to steal your girl."

Emerson and Taylah laugh in the background, used to his possessive habits.

"What are you doing here?" He holds out his hand, which I take and pulls me in for a one-armed hug. I choose not to answer him.

"Ladies, we are sorry to love you and leave you," I announce. "But we're going to head out and meet up with you both later."

Already aware of the plan, Taylah and Emerson give an unfazed response as they potter around the house getting ready to leave themselves.

"Did you all set this up?" Jagger asks, catching on.

"Yes. Can we go now?"

"What's the rush?"

"You're about two seconds off saying something that's going to make this very uncomfortable, and I would like to get out of here before it happens."

"This twin thing sucks. I was really going to embarrass you."

"I have no doubt. Now can we go?"

After a brief nod, he turns to Emerson, hugging and kissing

her goodbye. I take it as my cue to do the same and fold Taylah in my arms. "I'll see you soon okay?"

She tips her head up, welcoming my goodbye. The minute I feel her mouth on mine, I regret making plans. And when her tongue seeks out mine, I know she's thinking the exact same thing.

Jagger clears his throat, and I still waiting for his comment. "Was this how I was going to make it really uncomfortable?"

Embarrassed Taylah lowers her head, and I glare at Jagger. Lifting her chin up, I give her a quick peck. "Best weekend, remember."

With nothing but affection in her eyes, she repeats after me. "Best weekend."

"You've been too quiet for too long. Just say what you want to say already," I urge Jagger. We're fifteen minutes into the drive back to my place and he hasn't said a word since we got in the car.

"What do you want me to say?"

"Anything."

"That wasn't what I expected."

"What? Taylah and I?" I know he has something to say, but what shocks me is how much I want to hear it. I don't need his approval, but time and time again, I go seeking it, and I don't know why.

"No. Yes," he switches on a frustrated sigh. "I mean, I

assumed something was going to happen, you've brought her up enough the last few times we've seen each other. But I thought it would be a more of a feel-good time than what I just saw."

"What you just saw?" I echo with confusion.

"I've never seen either of you with other people, so I could be way off, but that looked a whole lot more than something casual."

It feels it too.

"I don't think it's casual," I admit to myself more than him.

He turns to me with curious eyes. "So you're really going there?"

The disbelief in his voice reminds me why I'm an idiot for having this conversation with him. "Do I have your permission?"

"That's not what I meant," he huffs. "I shouldn't have said what I said last week. You can be with whoever you want to be."

"Considering you didn't ask my permission before you slept with Sasha, I wasn't planning on listening to your warning anyway," I throw out angrily.

"That was low."

A small amount of guilt washes over me, but not enough to regret saying it. "It's still true."

After a few missed beats, he responds. "Hendrix, I'm sorry." He hangs his head in shame, his apology as sincere as ever.

"I know you are."

"Are you ever going to forgive me?"

"I forgave you the second I met Dakota, but some days I still find it really hard to forget."

We arrive in my driveway in silence, knowing words provide

little to no comfort. I lead us inside, throwing my keys on the dining table and heading straight to the kitchen for some coffee.

Hesitantly, he follows my footsteps. "Tell me about Taylah."

I wait for the drone from the coffee machine to slow itself down into a stop before answering. "What do you want to know?"

"What changed your mind?"

"She did."

"I just don't want shit to get even more fucked up for you."

"There's nothing *she* could do to make it worse." I bring the mug of hot coffee to my lips, embracing the scent of the hot liquid. "I feel good around her, and for the sake of just living in the moment, I'm going to see where it goes."

"You deserve to be happy."

"Then how come you fight me on every decision I make?"

He taps his fingers on the bench before saying whatever it is on his mind. "Honestly, I still can't get my head around you and Sasha not being together."

"Come on, bro. Even I've finally realised that ship has sailed."

"I just thought you'd be able to get past everything we went through."

"Me?" I run my hands through my hair in frustration. "When I lost the only family I had, grudges and heartache weren't options anymore. It was a clean slate for me. A lesson learned. She's the one that couldn't make it work."

"But why?" He's not expecting an answer to the question, but I do it anyway.

"Because Sasha is Sasha's worst enemy."

Each holding a cup of coffee, we spend a few minutes lost in the past and everything we endured to bring us to this point.

"For what it's worth, Taylah looks good on you."

Not wanting to spend the rest of the day at loggerheads, I help him out a little. "She really does look good *on* me."

He nudges my shoulder. "Are we good?"

"Yeah, bro. We're always good."

sixteen

TAYLAH

"Oh my God, you're actually alive," Emerson squeals. I roll my eyes at her theatrics before leaning in and giving her a one-armed hug. "I feel like I haven't seen you in forever."

"Relax, drama. It's been two weeks, and I've been busy." Sitting down opposite one another, I place my handbag on the chair beside me and start scanning the menu. "And, I've seen you at work."

"Please don't talk about that place," she cries. "I'm not loving it right now and I don't want to be reminded of it."

"Fuck, if I don't know that feeling too well."

"Yeah but I feel like your regular dates with the dick has gotten you through." She hides behind the menu, her eyes sparkle with mischief.

"Not gonna lie he makes the shitty days a lot better."

"Him or his dick?"

An innocent shrug and an accompanying smile gives her my answer.

Pushing back our weekly breakfast, Emerson and I finally managed to carve time in our schedule and catch up. While I have been really busy, Hendrix Michaels has become my addiction, and I'm not even sorry. After a great first weekend together, attached at the hip is an understatement.

There's no ruse, no rules, no games, and no worries. We're drowning, and neither wants to come up for air.

"You look like you're in love," she says, surprising me.

Shocked, I stay silent and ponder her statement. *Am I?*

"I'm happy."

"Tell me about him." She's excited and curious, a stark contrast from the original warning she gave me when I first mentioned taking a chance on Drix.

Avoiding her stare, I shut down her enthusiasm. "Not yet."

"What?"

After the awkward conversations both Hendrix and I have had with others about whether or not us together is a good idea, I tell her the honest truth. "I don't want to share this part of us with the rest of the world just yet."

Taken aback by my choice to keep something from her for the first time in history. I try to justify it. "Everyone had an opinion and I'm in too deep to hear them right now."

The rest of the morning takes a while to take off, and against both our wishes we end up talking about work.

Finishing off, we wait for the bill, before we make the already planned small walk from George Street to The Rocks, to check out the markets. Perusing the stalls is one of my favourite things to do. I've dragged Em all over Sydney before, hoarding one too many knickknacks. It's our thing and hopefully it bridges the gap I just created.

The waitress appears taking the money, only to leave the table, and make way for an unexpected sight.

"What are they doing here?" I ask, shocked to see Jagger and Drix walk in the café.

I watch every person's body turn as they head toward us. With each step, they fill the small and dainty space with masculine beauty. They're quite a pair, and if I wasn't satisfied knowing what it was like to have Drix in my own bed, I'd be jealous of anyone who had.

I glance over at Emerson, and her conflicted eyes find mine. "You did this?"

"You've been there for each of my happiest moments. I just don't want to miss out on yours."

I stretch my hands out to the middle of the table, and she does the same. "I love you."

"I love you too."

Giving my attention back to Hendrix, a loud sigh leaves my

mouth. "Does it ever wane?"

"What?"

"The need to want to be stuck to him at all times."

The look of yearning she gives Jagger answers my question. I turn my head, and my heart jolts to see Drix looking at me the same way. Impatient to greet him, I stand, and his strides show he feels the same.

"Fancy meeting you here." His large hands, cradle my face, as he leans in for a kiss.

My lips touch his, and talking seems overrated and unnecessary. He deepens the kiss, offering the smallest flick with his tongue, sending my body into a frenzy. I pull back, and look up at him, "I vote to never have to go out in public again."

His eyes twinkle with playfulness. "Sounds like the perfect plan to me."

Sliding my hands around his body, I lean my head against his chest and look at Emerson. I mouth thank you, equally grateful and guilty.

Her eyes dart from mine to Drix's, and back again. "It was a team effort."

Emerson tilts her head to the exit. "Ready to go?"

"You let us crash your day. We're good with whatever." Drix answers her, but he doesn't look at anything but me. I feel the bubble re-wrap itself around us, my worry gone; the rest of the world non-existent, just like I wanted.

Leaving the café, Emerson and Jagger lead the way, leaving

Drix and I trailing behind, arm around my shoulders, hand in his back pocket. "How was your morning with Jagger?"

"Not as good as being here with you now."

I pinch his arse through his jeans. "You're just so smooth aren't you."

"Jagger called me a miserable fuck and told me to call Emerson and organise to meet you. He was right. I fucking missed you." He kisses the top of my head. "It's a win win for all of us, I say."

Threading my free fingers into his, we fall into a comfortable silence. One where being in one another's presence far outweighs the need to justify our feelings with words.

As much as I love being in his arms, my shitty attitude to Emerson plays on repeat. "Can you give me a second?"

He narrows his eyebrows. "What's wrong?"

"I was a bit of a bitch to Em before and I just want to apologise one more time."

"What happened?"

"Can we talk about it later?"

"You know I won't forget."

I draw a cross over my heart. "I promise, I'll tell you."

He tips his chin at Emerson in front of us. "Go, make it better."

A row of white awnings come into view, the markets a continuous strip of stalls that serve everything from food, used books, jewellery, and clothes.

Feeling lighter, and less guilty, I take Drix's hand and lift his arm from around me. Skipping ahead, I tug at him to follow. "Come on, Sexy, we got things to see. Food to try."

"You trying to fatten me up?"

"Yes." I let go of his hand and walk backwards. "Just so I can have you work it off later."

His eyes breathe me in, as I indirectly promise he can use me to let it all out. "So, are you in or are you out?"

In two large steps his hands are on my waist, his forehead pressed to mine. "Can't we just browse casually like normal people?"

"And what would be the fun in that?" I place my hands on his chest, giving him a little nudge. "Here's what we're going to do. We go down the food aisle, and we each get a turn to feed the other."

He raises an eyebrow at me and clicks his tongue. "What's the catch?"

"Your eyes have to be closed."

"It sounds messy."

My hands latch behind the back of his neck, and I bring his face down to me. Tilting my head to the side, I whisper into his ear, "I promise I'll let you clean me up later."

We've been to more than ten food stalls, somehow falling into a pattern of only choosing desserts. Each stop became an experience my body and my mind wasn't prepared for.

I wanted to taste food, he wanted me to taste his lips. Sweet or sour, he convinced me everything tasted better this way. I lick the flavour off his lips, and he gives it back as he strokes the inside of my mouth.

It was all foreplay. He knew how to drive me wild with the simplest of touches. Public place be damned, he made sure I was lost in him, and I stayed where only he could find me.

"Okay. Okay. This is the last one," I announce. He starts to close his eyes, but I decide otherwise. "Keep them open for this." Tilting his head to the side, his facial expression questions what I have planned. I place the small caramel filled chocolate at the edge of my mouth, the other half poking out.

I move closer to his face, my intention clear. Or so he thinks. He leans in to bite the other half, but I move.

"What are you doing, Crazy?"

Without answering, I keep moving farther away. Chocolate in between my teeth, and a Cheshire Cat grin to match. It only takes Drix sixty seconds to be fed up, and catapult towards me.

A shriek leaves my mouth, leaving the chocolate to fall right out. His hands grip the front of my jeans and drag me to him. "You made me lose the chocolate," I pout.

"It's only fair," he shrugs. "You had no plans of sharing it."

"I think I can still taste it," I say, licking my lips.

"Yeah?" He moves closer, catching my bottom lip between his. "Mmmm. Tastes good," he moans. Sneakily he holds up the same caramel chocolate from earlier, and pops it in his mouth. He chews loudly, making animated noises. Looking smug and satisfied, he smirks at me. "Sorry Crazy, but this tasted way better."

Acting less like hormonal teenagers, and more like functional adults we walk through the aisles, and meet Emerson and Jagger at a handmade jewellery tent.

"Oh look," Em teases. "You guys decided to come up for air."

"You guys are just jealous you didn't think of it first," Drix retorts.

They bicker as we keep walking, and I'd be lying if I said it wasn't a relief that we'd all fallen into a comfortable exchange.

From the corner of my eye, I notice Jagger staring at me pensively. Unsure of what his problem could be I decide to walk ahead and check out some of my favourite stalls.

Expecting the figure beside me to be Hendrix, I'm surprised to see Jagger follow me.

Caught unaware and not sure what to say, I wait for him to break the silence. Bowed head, hands in pocket, he looks nervous as hell.

Surveying the wooden table in front of me, I graze my hand over the beautiful hand-woven bracelets. Picking one up, I turn to face Jagger, and hand it to him. "I don't bite, you know?"

Face to face, he takes my offering. His expression is stoic. Unreadable. A disparity to what comes out of his mouth. "I need to apologise."

I jerk my head back in shock. "Wait, what? What for?"

He rubs his hand over his mouth repeatedly as I wait for an

explanation. "Em told me what happened before we got to the café."

"Then why—"

"Wait." He holds his hand up in protest. "I need to get this out. I know you apologised to Em, and that's between you and her, but I should have *never* made you feel like that in the first place."

"Jagger. Stop." I place my hand over the hand that still holds the bracelet. "Please don't ever feel like you have to apologise for wanting to protect your brother."

"It's just." He arches his neck back, and takes a huge breath of air, clearly trying to compose himself. Eyes like Hendrix's look back down at me. A little older. A little more worn down. "There have been a lot of times in his life where he needed protecting, and I wasn't there. So now I overcompensate. Sometimes I'm rude and overbearing, but I promise my heart is in the right place."

His vulnerability chips away at the anger I held towards him for questioning our choices. I realise I can empathise with every shit turn their lives has taken, but I'll never really understand the after effects. I will never know what it's like to love and disappoint someone in the same breath, or be away from your family for so long, you've missed a lifetime. I will never know what it's like to be on the receiving end of that pain, and what it takes to learn to live with it.

And for that, I'm the one who should be apologising.

"Jagger, please let me say something."

"No," he says adamantly. "I know what you're going to say and it isn't necessary, because he's so fucking happy, and that's all you."

"No pressure. No expectation. No hard feelings if it just doesn't work out. Just a thank you." He tries to hand me back the bracelet. "You've taken good care of him."

I push the plaited fabric back into his hand. "That's where you have it all wrong. He doesn't need to be taken care off. He just needs to be set free."

Giving me a small nod, he swallows the lump in his throat, and looks down at the handmade jewellery.

"Oh." I clear my throat, getting rid of my emotions. "That's for Em. Buy it for her, she'll love it."

Keeping up with rituals I promise to text Em when I get home. Drix drives me and my car back to my place, both of us lost in our own thoughts. Me thinking about what Jagger said, him wondering what Jagger said. I feel overwhelmed with things I want to say and things I know I shouldn't.

Standing at the front door, strong arms wrap around me, cocooning me in. His mouth below my ear. "Are you going to tell me what you two spoke about?"

Giving him better access, I tilt my head, and unlock the door. "Let's go lay in bed."

"It's three o'clock in the afternoon." Refusing to let me go, we walk inside, attached to one another.

"You've got somewhere to be?"

"No," he growls as he nips my earlobe. "I just can't remember the last time I hopped into bed in the middle of the day."

"My dearest Hendrix, you haven't lived till you've jumped into bed for no other reason than because you can."

We step into my room, and he lets go of me. "I guess you'll have to teach me."

Walking to my newly designated side of the bed, I take off every stitch of clothing. No seduction. No purpose. I do it just because I can. Hopping under the covers, I turn my sheet covered body to the side. Resting my arm on the bed, I place my cheek on my palm. Looking up at Hendrix, I wave my free hand up and down, gesturing to his clothes.

"Do as you see, Padawan."

He strips naked, and jumps in beside me. Mirroring my pose, he asks me again. "Are you going to tell me what you two spoke about?"

Choosing to keep the long version to myself, I reveal the part that was most important. "He thanked me for making you happy."

It's a simple statement, but the weight of it isn't lost on either of us.

Tucking a few strands of my hair behind my ear, he leans forward and whispers in my mouth. "Thank you, Crazy."

I press my lips to his, giving him small pecks. Moving from the corner of his mouth to the side of his face and down his neck.

Pushing him to his back, I straddle him. Leaving kisses on his chest, down his stomach and back again. I feel the heat from his turned on body, light a match in my own.

With no words and no warning, I grab his stiff cock, and line it up with my entrance. Sliding myself down on him, he groans and I watch his face morph into tortured ecstasy.

Hovering over him, my hair falls like a curtain around us, emphasising our own little world. Movements cease, breathing is heavy. Feeling close and consumed, I wrap myself in his gratitude.

Like a feather tracing his lips, my mouth touches him with the utmost reverence. "Thank *you*."

seventeen

HENDRIX

Checking my watch, I estimate Taylah to be home any minute now. Since she had to cancel on dinner because of a work crisis, I figured I'd bring dinner to her. That, and she's now become like a drug to me. Close to fifty hours without seeing her and I'm desperate with need.

Her car turns into her driveway, the headlights beaming directly at me. I shield my eyes and wait for the car to turn off.

Blinded by the light, my eyes take several long blinks to adjust, my ears hearing her before I can see her.

"Hey," she says in surprise. "What are you doing, sitting out here in the dark?" She greets me with a kiss, before taking a seat beside me. She leans her head on my shoulder in exhaustion. I grab the plastic bag filled with food from next to my feet and pull it up to her line of sight. "I came to feed my girl."

"Your girl?" Her head perks up, and I can't help but smirk at her reaction.

"Is that okay?"

"Yeah..." she stammers. "I guess I didn't think of it."

It's all I've been thinking about.

"It's almost been a solid two months now, calling this anything else lessens it."

"Are you sure?" she asks skeptically, her reasons clear as day.

"I'm sure about how I feel about you."

I pray that my words reassure her, because they're the truth. Right now, there's nowhere else in the world I would rather be than by her side. Touching her. Talking to her. Laughing with her. She's fucking sunshine and I need her to warm up all the parts of myself I've left abandoned in the dark.

"Drix." Her voice soft and needy.

"Yeah."

"I'd be honoured to be your girl."

The relief within me is palpable. Curling my arm around her shoulders, I bring her even closer, and kiss her forehead. "Let's get you inside."

I walk into the kitchen, and set up our dinner on plates. Dropping her keys and laptop bag on the table, she unpacks her day; notebooks, manila folders and a shit load of pens.

"How was work?"

Walking toward me she takes the plate of fried rice, and spicy beef out of my hand. "Can we eat in bed and talk about it?"

"One of those days?"

She nods in defeat, leading me into her sanctuary.

Quickly changing into a t-shirt I've left behind, Taylah sits cross-legged on her bed and begins to eat.

Her mood is troubled, and while I hate knowing she's upset, being in her presence soothes my worry.

Following suit, I sit and eat, waiting for her to come out of her shell.

With all the time we now spend with each other, I've been able to pick out things about her that I would've never anticipated. Her ability to be so immersed in her job, she can't see past it, is one of them. Sometimes her empathy for others cripples her in a way I know exhausts her.

I admire her passion and her dedication, but the need to take care of her own wellbeing is something we always bicker about.

"Didn't you eat lunch today?" I ask as she shovels the food into her mouth.

She shakes her head. "By the time I had a few spare minutes, I just wanted to get the fuck out of there."

Looking down at her empty plate, I offer her the remainder of mine.

"No, you're still eating that," she protests.

"Eat, baby." I push it toward her again, taking her empty plate as encouragement. "There's more in the kitchen if I need it."

She devours the rest of my plate, and my heart does an

unexplainable dance, knowing she's eaten and full. "Let me get these to the kitchen, then we can talk about your day, huh?"

"Ughhh, do we have to?" She falls dramatically on to her bed.

"You're going to start talking about it in forty-five minutes anyway." She throws a pillow at me, and I laugh while blocking it with my shoulder. "I'll be back."

Returning to the room empty-handed, I notice she's swapped out the main bedroom light for her lamps. The television is on more as background noise, and she's managed to bury herself under a mountain of blankets.

I shuck off all my clothes, keeping only my boxer briefs on, and climb in next to her. Hooking my arm around her stomach, I bring her to me, her back pressing into my chest, our bodies curled up against one another.

"Today I managed to get the court to process an Apprehended Violence Order on a husband who beat the shit out of his wife and kid on the regular. He made bail, so the criminal charges will come later, but obviously the priority is to keep everyone safe."

My nose skims the length of her neck as my hand creeps up underneath her shirt; my skin desperate to feel hers. She talks, and I listen, giving her whatever she needs to feel better.

"He and his wife were selling anything and everything to score. We arranged for the mum to go into rehab with the hope she can eventually be reunited with her daughter."

"This young girl was just living her life. A victim to abuse, exposed to drugs, how do people do that around children? How do they expect them to grow up unfazed and unharmed."

Her voice trembles and all I can do is hold her tighter. "The part that gets me the most is how hard the young girl cried herself into an anxiety attack, because she wasn't going to see her parents again. They don't deserve her loyalty."

The picture forms perfectly in my mind, seeing it all the time at work. It's a battle that I wish we could win, but unfortunately, for the most part, families sometimes have to crack before they can be put back together. Turning in my arms, Taylah's wet eyes bore into mine and I wipe her escaping tears. "The thing about parents is we're programmed to love them no matter what. For a very long time, they're all we know. There are some parents, like yours who deserve superhero status. There are some who make the best with what they have. But for a lot of us, it's just a reminder we're all human and humans are not infallible. We make mistakes, and we're not perfect."

"Can I ask you something?"

"Of course."

"Why don't you ever talk about your mum?" She hooks her leg over my waist, bringing herself closer to me. "What happened?"

"She was a good mum in the sense that provided just enough for us. We had a roof over our head, shoes on our feet and food in our stomachs. But she was mean. If you ask me did she love us, I'd tell you I really don't know."

It's not until this moment do I realise how little I talk or even think of my mother. Unlike the rest of my past, she has no importance on my future. She's always been the one thing I've been happy to leave behind.

"After what happened with Jagger and Sasha…" Their names come out of my mouth as a pair before I can stop it, Taylah's face acknowledging it just as quick as I do. "Her tongue was razor sharp and she was on his case all the time. Constantly telling him that he and his kid would amount to nothing. I was so fucked up. I let her go to town on him." Placing her hand on the back of my neck, her fingertips draw circles on my scalp, the simple touch softening the memory. "He and I were just starting to get back on track before he went to jail, and when it happened, I finally understood how far she pushed him into proving himself."

Even though so much time has passed and I now get to see Jagger every day, the guilt for letting him get sucked into a false belief of unworthiness often eats at me.

"I couldn't forgive myself and I couldn't forgive her. As soon as I could, I was out of there."

"And now what?" she asks, every part of her engrossed in the story. "You don't speak to her or see her?"

"Not if I don't have to. I pay some of her bills, pay someone to maintain the house for her, and that eases my conscience."

"Does Jagger know?"

"He asked me about her when he got out, and I told him what I'd done. He offered to share her bills with me, but I refused."

"Why?"

I trace lines up and down her spine, her presence keeping me focused on the present and not the anger I'd spent so long holding against my mother for Jagger's incarceration.

"She was glad to see the back of him when he went inside. She never tried to see him or even asked me how he was, and her effort with Dakota was fucking dismal. For every person he might've needed to make it up to when he got out, she's not fucking one of them."

"Wow. I don't know what I expected, but that wasn't it."

"What do you mean?" Like she knows how much I love her body wrapped up in mine she clings tighter. Her core kissing my cock, her mouth inhaling my exhale, my eyes getting lost in hers.

"While the shit you've been through sucks, I can't get over how fucking selfless you are."

"I've always done what I have to do."

"You do that and then some." She brushes her nose against mine. "I know you didn't get it when you were growing up, and I doubt you let yourself hear it now, but you *are* an amazing person."

Hungrily, I snatch the praise out of her mouth. I let it roll around with our tongues, and let it flood me.

She forces herself off me mid-kiss. "I hope you're not trying to shut me up."

Shaking my head, I laugh, and kiss her again.

"I'm just saying thank you."

The mood around us changing, she grinds herself against me, my dick relishing in the attention. I slide my hand in between us and in the front of her underwear.

"You're always so fucking wet for me."

"It's only fair, you fuck me like nobody else."

Like the flick of a switch, I'm a man turned starved animal. Tugging at our clothes, I push inside her as quickly as I can.

The relief of unburdening myself of some of my past, mixed with Taylah's words washing over my skin, sends me into the ultimate high.

Rolling on top of her I pound her into the mattress. With every thrust, her body bounces. Her back arched and voice hoarse, I make sure she knows nobody will *ever* fuck her like this.

Quick, and raw, her pussy pulsates around me, and I fill her with everything inside of me. Good. Bad. Happy. Sad. I let her take it. I let her hold it. I let her heal it.

eighteen

TAYLAH

Finishing court early, I decide to see if Drix can spare an hour at work for lunch. Not wanting to wait till tonight to see him, I shoot a text through.

Me: *How's your day shaping up?*

Drix: *It's improving now.*

Me: *I finished court early, do you have time to spare for lunch?*

Drix: *Yes. The office will be empty by the time you get here.*

Me: *I'll buy something on the way.*

Drix: *Perfect.*

Traffic in the middle of the day is minimal, including a stop at a nearby café, I arrive at his office in just over thirty minutes.

Having not been there before, I follow the signs to where I think he would be, hoping to surprise him.

Ever since the adorable "my girl" declaration, everything feels different. Our bedroom fairy tale has turned into something tangible. Something I wasn't expecting. Something very real. Every day we get closer. Our hearts. Our minds. Our bodies. We're learning to live in each other's lives and it's the happiest I've ever been.

The door to what I assume is his office is ajar, and I nudge it open with my shoulder, my hands full with lunch. The sound of me entering has him looking up from his computer screen. Swapping his initial look of annoyance for a smile that shines in his eyes. "You're here."

Rising, he heads toward me as I mirror his steps. My eyes take in the graffitied walls and the sporadic places of other desks. "This place looks great."

Ridding me of the plastic bags, he places them on his desk before cupping my chin and bringing my face toward his. "You look better." His woodsy scent embraces me as my lips seek out his. "I don't think I tell you how much I love when you're dressed up like this."

I follow his eyes and look down at my high waisted pants and the tucked in camisole, covered with a short, three-quarter jacket. "I wear the same thing every day."

"No. On Court days everything is just that little bit sexier," he says bringing his thumb and forefinger close together. "Like you want to show everyone exactly who calls the shots."

"Does it work?" I ask playfully.

"Definitely." His lips part as he gives me a once over. "You look just as ruthless as you do beautiful."

"I knew there was a reason I kept you around."

"I thought it was my dick."

"And your compliments." Excited to finally be in Drix's workspace, and see another part of his world, I step away and give myself a mini tour. "So, where is everyone?"

"Most of them are out at the local schools, checking up on all their clients." He explains the ins and out of the place as he sets up our lunch across his desk. "I try to schedule my outside visits when everyone is in the office, so it's a little bit quieter, and the majority of my clients are kids you won't find in school."

I hear the sandwich wrappers rustle behind me. "Are you coming to eat?"

"Just give me a second," I call back to him. "These walls are fucking brilliant."

"They are. There are some fucking talented kids out there."

I look back at him. "Your clients did this?"

"Yeah. Every two years we let them revamp it for us. If they create the space, they respect it more, and in turn respect what you're trying to do for them."

"You love working here, don't you?"

The side of his mouth lifts in a smirk. "Am I that obvious?"

I let the smile stretch across my face, hoping my eyes convey how proud I am to know a man who is so passionate about the welfare of others. As obvious as it sounds to help someone in need, it is not in everyone's nature to do so. The world is blessed with hearts like Hendrix's to make the losses and injustices a little easier to bear.

Someone will always remember the shitty time in their life, but they'll remember the one who offered to help them when they needed it most even more.

Engrossed in the art, I give Drix my back and trace the designs with my hands. "Do you ever just want to take these kids home and give them a proper chance?"

"All the time," he says with no reservation. "It was harder when I first started, because I wanted to save the world. Now I'm less green and understand the system and the kids much more. But every now and then I'll meet one person who will blow my mind, and I just let myself imagine the possibilities."

"I think that's what I want to do one day, open my house up and foster kids."

"What about kids of your own?" he asks, the view of my back making it easier for me to answer.

"I mean I want them, I guess. I'd just have to have the right partner." Like a flash of lightning, a vision of Drix with our baby hits me with a pang of longing in my chest. "What about you?"

"I haven't had a reason to think of myself as a father in a really long time." The admission has me reading between the lines, wondering if he ever wished Dakota was his. "But I believe compatibility and unity is everything. As old school as it sounds, I want to be with the mother of my baby. I want to be sure it's forever."

Could that be me?

"Coming from a broken home and watching Dakota grow up without a dad," he continues. "It's become my one single requirement."

"And the foster kids?"

"That's an added bonus." I hear his chair squeak before footsteps sound in my direction. "If I have the means to provide for as many kids as possible, why wouldn't I?"

If in that moment anybody asked me what Hendrix's most attractive quality was, I'd tell you his heart. His huge, selfless and pure heart.

"Please come and eat," he whispers unexpectedly in my ear.

"I can't stop looking at it." What I really mean is the broken beauty on these walls makes me think of missed opportunities. It makes my heart heavy for all the things their lives could be. And it has me desperately wanting to make a difference.

"When it's time to change the space, you could come here and draw with them. Show them how good you are."

Merged with my thoughts of him and I having babies together and a house full of foster kids, his slip about the future hits me like a boulder to the chest. It makes me nervous, and excited, and so fucking relieved that I'm not the only one that's falling hard and fast.

Leaning back, I relax into him and take one last look at the wonders in front of me. "I'd love that."

"So, I've got something I want to ask you." Drix looks at me over the table, a hint of trepidation passes his features.

"What is it?"

"It's Dakota's sixteenth birthday next weekend and she's having a thing at Jagger's." He fidgets with his earlobe, his own uneasiness spurring on mine. "And, I want you to come with me."

"Oh." The invitation is unexpected, and my gut tells me there are a million reasons why I shouldn't go. It's a beautiful gesture, one that screams, family, importance, future, and love. Everything a woman wants to hear and feel from the man she's with, but this isn't a conventional situation, and I don't know if our bubble is strong enough to withstand the intrusion.

"Say something," he urges.

Pinching my bottom lip between my fingers, I line up the sentence in my mind before I blow all the progress we've made. "Are you sure it's a good idea with Sasha being there?"

"I don't know."

"I'm sorry, but that's not enough Drix." He watches me pensively, as I continue. "If you want me to meet Dakota, as your girlfriend, we can do it on our own time, but I'm not ruining that girl's birthday party."

"Who said anything about ruining it?"

"Come on, you know better than that." I run my hands up and down my thighs, trying to contain my nervous energy. "She threw shade my way when the idea of us hadn't even been conceived yet. What do you think she'll do when she finds out we're together?"

"We're all adults, Taylah," he says condescendingly. "And we've been playing nice for Dakota our whole lives."

His lack of concern and my unsure heart has me biting back. "How do I know you don't want me there to shove it in her face?"

Closing the distance between us, he comes around from the desk, kneeling in between my legs.

His voice cracks. "Where is this coming from?"

Lowering my head, I let my hair hide my face. "You've loved her forever, Drix. I know those words haven't come out of your mouth, but I know," I insist. "And I can't compete with that. Not now, not when we're still so new."

He doesn't run to my defence and tell me he isn't in love with her anymore or tell me there's no competition between us. It leaves a little scratch on my heart as I feel like our whole relationship just stepped back in time.

"I told you once and I'll say it again." My voice is low and steady, the anger brewing within me. "I will not be your practice girlfriend."

"Crazy." He shakes his head. "You've got it all wrong."

"Do I? Because you haven't said anything to make me think otherwise."

He splays his hands on either side of my face, bringing me so close to his face, our noses are touching. "I asked you because I want you to come, because I want you there. To be part of the things and people that are important to me. I didn't ask you so you can question everything between us."

Grabbing his wrists, I pull his hands down, off my face. I put my heart on a plate and hand it to him. "I'm falling in love with you, Drix. Please don't make me regret coming to this party."

His mouth opens, but a different voice makes itself known throughout the reason. "Ah, shit, sorry Drix, I can come back later."

"No. No. It's okay." Holding on the arms of the chair, he gets up off his knees. "Come in and have a seat."

His client walks in with his head down, embarrassed and uncomfortable. Standing up, I right my clothes, and throw my bag over my shoulder.

"Can we talk more about it later?" Drix asks me quietly.

"No. It's fine." I squeeze his shoulder. "I said I would come. So I will."

"I'll see you tonight?" he asks, and for the first time in a long time, my answer changes.

"I'll call you tomorrow."

He glances between me and the kid, knowing very well this isn't the time or the place to argue. Knowing I backed him into a corner, I leave the room well aware he can't come after me.

As I'm just about to exit the room, I hear the young boy say, "You fucked up, Drix."

I still in the doorway when I hear his response.

"I know, man. I know."

nineteen

HENDRIX

I drop on to Jagger's couch, a little worse for wear after setting up a marquee in the afternoon heat for Dakota's birthday. He hands me a cold beer before taking a seat on the opposite recliner.

"Those kids better stay under the marquee the whole time," Jagger jokes. "It's only fair after how hard it was to put that fucker up."

"It's not their fault they didn't teach you how to use basic tools in prison."

"Shut the fuck up," he scoffs while throwing the beer bottle cap directly at my head. "There was nothing basic about that thing."

"It's fine, I get it, we can't be good at everything," I tease. "Next time just bloody well pay for someone."

"I just wanted to do something for her, myself, you know?"

His tone steers the conversation back to all the ways he thinks he falls short.

"Yeah, bro, of course, I was just kidding."

"I know you were," he says dismissing my comment. "I just think this whole birthday thing means more to me than it does to her."

I want to tell Jagger that Dakota has never gone a day without in her life, and having her father be there is the gift. All the other shit we give to kids is just extra bells and whistles to fulfil our own materialistic needs. However, no matter which way I word that, the message I'm trying to get through to him is not the one he will receive.

It's never my intention to throw in his face all the time I've had with her, and I'm cautious not to. Our lives have come so far beyond tit for tat on who sacrificed the most.

He missed watching his daughter grow up, and I raised a girl who would never be mine. These thoughts are selfish and destructive. Secrets, he and I promised to keep in the vault.

We've come so far from the volatile people we were to one another back then. I try not to remember the bad days, the fights, and all my regrets.

"Bro, can I come in?"

"Yeah." Shoulders hunched over my desk I finish the mountain of homework that I get lost in every week. "What's up?" I glance up at Jagger and I'm immediately thrown off by the way he looks. Jittery and nervous are not words I would ever use to describe my brother. "What's wrong?"

He walks into the room and sits on the edge of my bed. "I need to tell you something."

"Okaaayyy." I push off my desk and spin my chair to face him.

"I need you to know I'm really really sorry." His voice trembles, his eyes begin to water, and I'm at a loss at what the fuck could be the problem.

Out of habit, I roll the desk chair toward him, offering comfort. "Jagger, man, whatever it is, it can't be that bad."

He's shaking his head vehemently, working himself up by the second. "Tell me you'll forgive me."

I lean my hand on his shoulder, "Of course I'll forgive you."

"Are you sure?"

"Yes, man. Spit it out."

He closes his eyes and takes a big breath before letting it out in one large whoosh. When he opens them, he stares directly at me. "Sasha is pregnant."

For a second my mind just shuts down, unable to mentally process the three words he just dropped on me

"She's pregnant," I repeat, rolling the words on my lips, trying to shut the images down from my mind. "I'm going to kill that piece of shit." Loud. Angry. Hurt. There isn't a spare corner in my room that can't feel my wrath. I jump up out of my chair and pull my hoodie over my head. "Are you coming or what?"

"Where?" he asks, looking perplexed.

"I'm going to find Jay, and beat the shit out him."

"You know about Jay?"

"Yeah man," I say impatiently. "I knew when she started hanging with him, and then she and I had a blow up about it long after."

"How long ago?"

I look up at my calendar. "About six weeks now."

"Drix, sit back down," he pleads.

"What the fuck, man?"

"It's mine," he screams, window shatteringly loud.

"Come again?" My voice is so low, the contrast between him and I frightening.

"We were at Lachlan's party. Remember I asked you to come?" he rambles, and I'm frozen in time. "But you were too busy turning into a fucking church monk." The room begins to spin while he continues to spew out his confession. "She was so upset, and I was already so fucking trashed. I told her to try and talk to you about Jay. I did. That's what I thought she was upset about. That's what she said to me."

"So, she came to you crying," I seethe. "And you fucked her?"

"Dr—"

I don't hear my name, I don't see his face, I can't hear him shouting. I race at him, elbow into his stomach, I ram him back into the bed. Gripping the collar of his shirt in one fist, I pull back my arm and let his face meet the other.

I don't stop. I can't stop. And he takes every single hit.

"Are you keeping it?" I spit out, through angry tears.

"Yes." Instinctively he tries to duck, knowing my next move, but he fails.

Arms grip me from behind, my mother's voice breaking through.

"What the fuck is going on here?"

I finally let him go and stumble backwards into my mother's arms. I wipe my bloodied knuckles on my shirt. "Why don't you ask Jagger?"

"Well come on, let it out. I don't have all fucking day."

As horrible as my mother was, you never kept her waiting. Unable to look at me or her, he confesses his biggest secret while his blood drips on my floor. "I slept with Sasha."

Mum uses the opportunity to bask in her favourite past time; screaming at Jagger.

"You're a fucking useless piece of shit, you are. You can't keep your damn dick in your pants." She doesn't skimp on the insults, and for the first time in history, I let her keep going. "I said don't be like your father, but here we are, sticking it in any hole that fits."

"This is between me and Drix." He stares at me while she yells at him. A messed up version of myself looks at me, begging me for forgiveness. And I've got nothing to give.

"You didn't tell her the best part," I taunt. "They're having a baby. You're going to be a grandmother."

"He better be fucking lying, Jagger."

He hangs his head in shame. "Drix, I'm so sorry," he cries.

"Get out of my room," I say calmly.

He steps up beside me, "I'm not going until you forgive me."

"Get out of my fucking face before I kill you."

He closes the rest of the distance between him and the door. "I'm going to make this better."

One brother beaten, and the other broken. "Don't bother, you and

I can't be fixed."

Pulling myself out of the painful memory, I take a long swig of my beer, grateful that's in the past and more focused on reminding Jagger, the party will be everything him and Dakota need. It will fall into place, and she'll hold the memory as close as the rest of the things she cares about.

"Where's Em? I thought she'd be here fussing over the decorations with you."

"No," he says, averting his eyes, and picking at the beer label. "She's with Taylah. Some emergency."

"Oh."

"I hate to point out the obvious, but shouldn't you know that?" I take another drink, not really having any actual answers to what's going on in my life right now.

I know I've hurt her, I know she's confused, I just don't know how to fix it. "I know what the emergency is."

He looks at me pointedly. "Well?"

"I asked her to come tomorrow." I stretch my arm out, place the empty beer bottle down. "And it brought up a whole bunch of shit that I didn't even see coming."

"Sasha?"

"The one and only." Leaning to the right, I angle my body till I'm lying down on Jagger's couch. "I mean, seeing Sasha tomorrow was in the back of my mind, but spending a day here without Taylah seemed wrong."

With my hands behind my head, I stare at the ceiling and

hope Jagger can help me sort out this mess.

"She told me she was falling in love with me, and I didn't say anything back." The look on her face when she said those words, tears through my chest. Every night since I've wished I could turn back time and redo the whole conversation. I should've said it back, because in my heart I feel it. It's more than like, and it's way past lust. I was just too wrapped up in the newness of it all to realise love is what comes next.

It would be a lie to say I wasn't nervous about Sasha and Taylah being in the same room together. It would be a lie to say I don't love Sasha anymore. Truth is, I don't know. I chose to keep my distance and live my life. Does that make everything else go away?

"You know what?" I get up off the couch and walk our empty beer bottles to the kitchen. "I'm lying here on your furniture like I'm in a fucking therapist's office when I just need to go to her place and talk to her."

I've been pussyfooting around her and our issues all week, not wanting to make it worse, but if I don't clean out the wound, it won't heal. Opening his front door, I look back at Jagger who is watching me with mild amusement. "I'll see you tomorrow, okay, bro."

"Tell Emerson I'm waiting for her," he calls out.

He means his dick is. Gross.

"Just fucking sext her like a normal person."

Standing on her porch, I knock on the fly screen waiting for her to answer. I don't think I've ever stood here this long, her hands usually dragging me in before my foot has even touched the first step.

Opening the door, she doesn't look too shocked to see me.

Fucking Jagger.

A little fragile, and a little defeated, she stares at me with the same questions she's had all week.

"Can I come in?"

Emerson's head pops into view. "Of course you can," she answers for Taylah. "I was just leaving."

They say a quick goodbye before the screen door opens, and Em gives me a quick peck on the cheek and heads off home.

I step in, and Taylah steps back. "What are you doing here?"

Hesitant and unsure, she wraps her body with her cardigan. Crossing her arms across her chest, she adds another barrier between us.

"I came to see you."

Again, I move forward, and she moves back. "Why do you keep doing that?"

"If you touch me, I can't think. I won't be able to remember why I'm mad, why I'm scared and why I'm confused." Her shoulders are stiff, and her right leg bounces on the spot. She's in knots and it's all my fault. "If you touch me, I'll crumble."

"You haven't let me touch you or see you in a week." I shrug.

"I miss you."

The distance felt significant when we spoke on the phone during the week, but in person, it feels irreparable.

"I know." She nods. "I miss you too."

Pushing my fingers through my hair, I pull at the tips. "Tell me what to do. I want to fix this."

"You're going to go home, and give me tonight." Her voice is cool and calm, a complete one-eighty from her body language. "Tomorrow, come and pick me up, and everything will be okay."

"No," I say strongly. "No. Things don't get better if you ignore them. Everything you've been feeling won't just magically disappear in the morning." I school my breathing. Tapering the frustration coursing through me. "I came here to speak about it."

"I don't want to speak about it," she argues.

"I'm going to speak," I say, pointing at my chest. "I just need you to listen."

She hugs herself tighter, and the fact that she won't let me comfort her makes my skin unbearable to be in. "Last week when you told me you were falling in love with me, I should—"

"Don't," she shouts. "I am *not* mad because you didn't say it back."

Choosing my words carefully, I tell her my heart has every intention of falling with hers. "What I was going to say is if there's anyone in the world made to put the pieces of my heart back together and cherish it, it's you." I swallow the lump in my throat and continue. "I'm sorry I didn't clarify that you are important to me. I should've told you that you're not a practice girlfriend.

That you're not a stand-in. I should've told you that you're not replaceable. And above all else, you. *Are*. Mine."

If I was unsure about how I felt, seeing her in flight or fight mode, kicked me into gear. I have a past. I have scars, but if I'm not careful, I'm going to lose my future.

"Tomorrow, it's your turn to tell me about it, okay?" She acknowledges my request, but something has me still uneasy that she's trying to say goodbye. "Promise me I'll see you tomorrow," I demand.

Silence.

"Say it."

A lone tear rolls down her face. "I promise."

twenty

TAYLAH

I stare at myself for the last time making sure my puffy eyes are covered and I've practiced my fake smile enough times even I believe it.

It's morbid, and one hundred percent inappropriate, but I've spent the week mourning my relationship with Drix, but last night, through all the hurt, his words sparked hope.

Today will be my fresh start. For Drix, I will put my big girl panties on and face the woman that holds my future in her hands, and I will take it back.

Because she can't have him. And if she tries. I'm not going down without a fight.

My phone dings with a text, and sure that it's Drix telling me he's close, I give myself a quick once over in the full-length mirror.

Perfect.

Grabbing my clutch, I slip my shoes on and walk down my front steps. Leaning on the passenger side door is the man I've fallen in love with. His feet are crossed and arms are folded, he looks *light and casual*.

Standing in front of him, I wear my shyest smile. "Hi."

"Fuck saying hi." Grabbing me by the waist, he lifts me up high enough to wrap my legs around him. Turning, he pushes me into the door and obliterates every kiss before this one. "Don't ever keep these from me again," he murmurs in my mouth. "Got it?" He grips my arse through my dress and presses me into his solid length. A loud moan is my answer.

"I promise to finish this later."

Flushed and turned on, I nod as my body slides down his. Opening the door, he helps me get into the car; groping me any chance he gets.

Waiting for him to jump in, I pull my phone out and find a song. As if the last seven days didn't happen, we fall into sync. "You going to sing for me, Crazy?"

I hit play on "Your Mess is Mine" by Vance Joy, and wink at him. "Always."

He finds my hand and weaves his fingers through mine as the words of the song settle between us. The song ends only to start up again, and he glances over at me with a raised brow.

"I know how much you love them on repeat." He lifts my hand to his lips.

I love you too.

Remembering to tell Drix something, I lower the volume and pull a slim length envelope out of my bag. "I forgot to tell you I bought Dakota a gift from us."

"Yeah? What did you get her?"

"Well, the Museum of Contemporary Art is holding a photography exhibition in a month. They're all up and coming photographers, and I figured the three of us could go."

My heart beats frantically, wondering if I've overstepped, but the heart-stopping smile on his face is the reassurance I need. "She's going to love that."

"I think so."

He pulls into the driveway, and a wave of nausea hits me. I countdown from twenty and pray an overactive imagination has me exaggerating the whole thing.

"We're going to be okay," he says, noticing my mood change.

"I know." Releasing a loud breath, I open the door and wait for Drix to help me from the car.

And who said chivalry is dead.

With the usual arm around my shoulder and my hand in his back pocket, we walk in the front door. Top forty music plays on the stereo as Dakota and a hand full of boys and girls are scattered throughout different areas of the house. The kitchen bench is lined with different types of party food. It's probably my favourite thing about kid parties. Bite-sized goodness.

With no other adults in sight, Drix leads us to a dressed up

Dakota. Swapping out her everyday jeans and tank for a beautiful spring dress, she looks every bit the sixteen-year-old girl she is.

Her friends notice us first, a few of them blatantly crushing on the cool uncle. One by one they stop talking, waiting for their friend to realise she's got company.

Eventually picking up on the clues, she turns around, her eyes shining with happiness as they land on Drix.

"Uncle Drix," she squeals. "You're here."

We let go of one another and he lowers half his body to kiss her on the head. "Where else would I be?"

She looks from between him and I. "T, I didn't know you were coming."

Knowing she doesn't mean it any which way, I shrug it off and stick my hand up for our traditional high five greeting. "It's not every day someone turns sixteen."

Drix clears his throat, all our attention back to him. "Kid. I actually invited Taylah here, as my girlfriend."

He drops the bomb, and I wait for her response, except she isn't the one who speaks.

"Did you just say your girlfriend?" The voice is familiar, and the shock is evident.

"This is so great," Dakota cries. "Mum, can you believe Uncle Drix has a girlfriend? I was sure he was going to be single forever."

The temperature in the room drops significantly as we all come face to face with one another. I realise Dakota doesn't know about her mum and Drix, and this just got one hundred times more awkward. She's so happy for him. Sasha is about to lose her mind, and everybody else is a spectator.

"We've moved the party under the marquee, to please Jagger," Emerson shouts out. "How about you all come outside and leave the adults inside."

Without a second glance the kids file in a line outside and Emerson closes the thick glass sliding door.

Expecting more drama, I'm shocked to see Sasha walk straight outside with the kids.

I turn to Drix, but he's watching Sasha, and my heart breaks.

I try not to take it too personally, or to expect too much from him. I have an empathetic heart, and for him, I can understand the difficulty of seeing someone you care about in any capacity hurt.

But I'm here, and he hasn't once asked if I'm okay.

Emerson's eyes lock with mine, the sympathy written on her face has me wanting to run into her arms and cry.

"Do you need help with anything?" I ask, begging her to take to the bait.

"Uh, yes. Actually, can you just man the oven for a while." She points at random boxes behind her. "Just take the food out and put the new stuff in."

"Got it." Unable to bring myself to look anywhere else but Emerson, I bolt straight to the kitchen.

Losing track of time, I don't know how long I've been in front of this oven. All I know is Drix hasn't come to find me once. Last night I felt every single one of his words in the marrow of my bones. Today, he's a stranger.

I see him outside with the kids, keeping a close eye on them, pretending they need him more than I do. Sasha continues to be the perfect host for her daughter's party, acting like she wasn't the one who lit the fuse on my relationship.

"Are you okay?" Emerson asks, interrupting my seething. "I'm so sorry I keep leaving you alone in the kitchen."

"Don't be silly. Do your thing, I'm fine here." Truth is I couldn't muster a conversation without falling apart anyway. I'll wait til Dakota blows the candles out on her cake and then I'm out.

Setting up another few trays full of frozen party food, I slide on the oven mitts and make the swap. From the corner of my eye, I see Sasha corner Drix. It takes everything I have not to walk out of this kitchen and find out what she has to say. Her hands are flailing and his mouth is moving.

They're mad, and if they're not careful, the rest of the guests are going to notice, and they're going to ruin Dakota's birthday. She looks over to them. Once. Twice. Three times. My feet move like they have a mind of their own, and I'm heading straight towards them like an arrow to its mark.

"Be with me." Those are the only words I hear her say, and

like a ticking time bomb, I'm ready to explode.

Coming into their vision, their guilty faces are like stab wounds to my already broken heart.

"Taylah." He says my name with shock, like he may have just remembered he came with someone.

Sasha looks at me square in the eyes, and I give her my very best smile. "While I'm not a fan of either of you right now, Dakota is about three seconds from coming here and making your problems hers. It's her birthday. So get the fuck inside like the adults you're *supposed* to be and sort your shit out, out of her sight."

Their heads immediately turn to her, and just like I said Dakota's worried eyes stare right back at them.

Leaving them behind, I walk up to Dakota and her friends in hope of lightening up the mood. She glances past me one more time, but they've already disappeared inside.

"Are they okay?" she whispers.

"Yep. They were just arguing because we accidentally bought you the same gift as your mum, and they both really want to take you."

"Really?" She's sceptical, but I keep going.

"Tickets to that amateur photo exhibition at MCA. Have you heard of it?"

"Oh my God," she gasps. "Are you serious? Please tell me you're not joking."

"I am definitely not joking."

She looks back around the backyard, her untainted heart

worrying till the last second.

Standing up I give her shoulder a soft squeeze. "They're okay, D. I promise."

Dreading the walk back inside, I decide it's time for me to leave. I'm Emerson's friend. Nothing more, nothing less. I don't need to be here.

Stepping back inside, Jagger's wide eyes greet me. "What?"

He looks at Dakota's bedroom door and I take it as my cue. "Thanks for having my back, J."

Holding the door handle, I give myself five seconds to back out. Five seconds to save myself from seeing something I'm never going to forget. Five seconds to walk out of this house with enough pieces of my heart to maybe, one day be able to put it back together.

twenty one

SASHA

I saw red the minute I noticed her in the house. For a fleeting second, I thought how if it was my house I would have been able to ask her to leave.

He did it. He went and did the exact thing I've been begging him to do for years. The exact thing that I wanted, but prayed it never happened. He moved on.

It's my daughter's birthday. I have kept it together for all these years, today is not the day I break.

Floating around through the kids, I offer them food and drinks and watch them dance.

When I was sixteen, I had a baby. My friends were getting drunk at their own or someone else's sixteenth, and there were even the few appearances from the kids we called the stoners.

This is nothing like that, and I couldn't be happier.

"Mum," Dakota's voice travels through the people and straight to my ears.

"Yes, baby girl."

"Can you please take a photo of me with everyone, with my new camera."

"Of course. Let me just free up my hands." I head on inside with an empty tray of cheese and dips. Sliding it on the kitchen bench, I come face to face with Taylah.

Surprisingly, she doesn't glance my way.

Hiding in the kitchen, she hasn't said a single word to anyone. Including Hendrix.

Pleasantries are not even an option at this stage, the long and firm line drawn between us, cannot be erased. One woman on each side. One woman claiming her own part of him. One woman who'll have him. One woman who won't.

Washing my hands, I make sure any excess food residue has one hundred percent been cleaned before I touch Dakota's pride and joy. Not only is she meticulous about who touches it and how, when you've spent as much as I have on camera paraphernalia you want to make sure their condition stays pristine for a very. Long. Time.

I make my way through the guests. Each photo I take, Dakota's smile gets bigger, and my heart wants to break out from my chest in pride.

She takes a photo with Emerson and Jagger, Jagger and Drix and then the two of them by themselves. When Dakota finally decides on a pose and orders me around with requests about the angle of natural lighting, I capture their sixteen years of unconditional love. From the beginning, I wondered what their relationship would be like. Whether he would hold my mistakes against her, or if she would be the reason he gave me a second chance.

I see the way he looks at Dakota, and I excitedly anticipate the idea of having children of our own. We're older now, but we're not too old to start a whole new life together. Guilt and pain free.

I pretend that the photo isn't coming out right and take a few more. My thoughts run into the future, thinking maybe this is when the stars finally align. I'm ready, and I know deep down inside he will forgive me one more time. For the last time.

Putting the camera down, Dakota bounces to her friends and he's left alone, cornered by me, and with nowhere to go. Determined to get to our happy ever after, I make it my mission to wade through all the bullshit first.

"So, you and Taylah, huh?" I try to be unaffected by the acidic taste left in my mouth after saying their names together. "I'd like to say it was a surprise, but we both know I saw it coming."

"What do you want, Sasha? Once and for all just spit it out." Exasperated his words come out through clenched teeth. "Please."

"Be with me." More important than the other three words he's said to me a million times. These are the key to our future.

"I'm sorry, what did you just say? I could've sworn you said be with me, but that can't be right." Laced with sarcasm and hurt, I feel the years of rejection take its toll on him. "Sasha, you need to stop playing games. This isn't fun anymore."

"I'm not playing at anything," I shout defensively. "Be with me."

As the demand leaves my mouth, Taylah comes into view. Her jaw clenched, a fake smile plastered on her face, as she warns us we're about two seconds from ruining Dakota's birthday.

Drix storms off muttering to himself and Taylah heads over to Dakota. Weighing up my options, I follow Drix. There's no time like the present.

Slamming Dakota's bedroom door, Drix and I stand in the middle of her room, waging war. "You did this the last time you saw me with Taylah. Stop. Doing. It."

Ignoring his warning, I let it out. I tell him how I feel. "I'm ready, Drix."

His eyes dart to mine, and I know the statement does exactly what it was meant to.

Said to me by a broken boy with the promise he made me in his darkest hour. I repeat the one thing that will bring him home.

Sitting up in the treehouse, I wait for Drix to meet me. Not expecting him to show, I'm rewarded with three knocks on the makeshift wooden door.

Scoping out the space he looks for the farthest corner in the room and makes his way to sit there. Knees up, shoulders hunched over, he's hurt and defeated.

Knowing about what happened with him and Jagger, I jump straight into the mess. There's nothing left to sugar coat, and I don't deserve it to be.

"I'm keeping the baby," I inform him of my decision, even though

he knows me well enough to expect that anything else wasn't an option. "It's Jagger's."

The silence fills up the box-like space, like water rising. It pushes me under, making it harder to focus. Harder to breathe.

"Say something, Drix."

Shaking his head, he stares out the window. "I've got so much to say, Sasha, but none of it changes anything."

"Why aren't you mad?" I push. "You beat the shit out of Jagger, why aren't you screaming and shouting at me?"

"Like I said, it doesn't change anything."

"Can I sit next to you?" Placing my hands on the floor, I give myself a push, only to see his head shaking in my direction. The answer expected, but still painful.

"I'm sorry. I'm so so sorry."

"I was furious about Jay. Fucking furious," he spits out. "You were there when you told me, you got the full brunt of my reaction."

I chose to tell Drix about Jay, because I knew he would be sharing his conquest with the world any minute. I could predict Drix finding out, and him losing his mind, just like he did with Jagger.

"But I'm still trying to work out how me being so mad pushed you into sleeping with Jagger?"

I wish I had an explanation. I wish I had a good enough reason to make all this worthwhile, but I don't. I just have a long list of mistakes, because I was too immature and too insecure to let myself enjoy anything in life.

"It wasn't intentional. I was so upset, and it just happened," I try

to explain. "I'm so, sorry."

"Stop saying fucking sorry," he yells. "Do you even mean it when you say it? Do you?" His fury is all it takes for slow tears to turn into an uncontrollable sob. He looks up at me for the first time, his eyes full of nothing but hate. "I feel like I don't know you at all. You've done almost everything there is to push me away and break my heart."

"I'm sorry I'm such a disappointment," I bite back through tears, my defence mechanism trying to push through.

"It's like you decided to sleep with everyone who wasn't me," he says flippantly.

"Are you calling me a slut?"

"Don't twist my fucking words." His lips curl up in disgust. "You broke up with me because you thought I wanted sex, and you *weren't ready. Yet here I am, the only virgin in the room."*

"Will you ever forgive me?"

"You're having my brother's baby."

"You'll be an uncle." I cringe as soon as the words make their escape "Shit, I—"

"What an awesome consolation prize," he scoffs. Pushing on his knees, he rises and walks toward me. Kneeling in front of me, he grabs my hands. "It should've been mine, Sasha. Right now, or ten years from now we should've been having children together."

"We still can," I whisper.

"Maybe one day when the dust settles and the stars align you and I can have our life together."

"Yes," I cry. "We can Drix, I know we can."

"But for now." The slight bit of hope I heard in his voice only two seconds earlier disappears quick smart. "I don't want to see your face, or hear your voice. I want it to be like you don't even exist."

THE BIRTH OF DAKOTA

Laying on my chest, I check her hands and feet, and make sure all her fingers and toes are there. Skin on skin, I'm exhausted, she's content and every single thing in my life before this moment pales in comparison.

It's been a day since I gave birth to her, and as each hour passes, I'm even happier than the one before. Jagger has slipped into his role with ease, the love and adoration he has for this delicate new life, mirroring mine.

The door opens, and I expect to see Jagger or the nurse come in to check up on me, but it's Drix.

Scraping a chair across the carpet, he sits beside me, his eyes all on her. "She's beautiful," he says in a hushed tone.

It's been almost a year and I've managed to stay out of his way, exactly like he asked. Shocked, I lay back and enjoy hearing his voice.

"I know you're tired. So just listen, okay?"

Nodding, I close my eyes, the onslaught of emotions from seeing him, mixed with my hormones, too much to bear. "This has been the hardest and happiest moment of my whole life, but I want it."

My heart slams against my chest.

"I want it with you, Sasha." His finger wipes the one rogue tear I couldn't hold in. "When the dust settles and the stars align, tell me you're ready, and I'll be waiting."

twenty two

HENDRIX

"I'm ready, Drix."

The hushed words dance around my ears and tickle my mouth. "You can't say that now. It's not fair."

"It's true." Her knuckles caress the side of my face. "When all the dust settles, and the stars align. I. Am. Ready."

Her lips skate across mine, and I wait for the usual rush of greed, desperation, and hunger to follow.

It doesn't come.

Where's Taylah?

twenty three

TAYLAH

I watch him step away from her, but her lips on his, for even a split second still hurts. They're mine.

They both look at each other shocked. I expect it to change to guilt the minute they see me in the room but whatever was exchanged has shaken them enough not to notice me.

"Drix." My shaky voice catches both of their attention, but I don't give anyone but Drix mine. He turns my way, the light from his eyes missing, his brows furrowed in confusion.

His breath becomes louder, more laboured. The rise and fall of his chest has me confused to whether he's angry or anxious. Dashing over to him, I walk him back to the bed. He sits, and I kneel down in front of him. "Drix, baby. Just breathe. In. Out."

He follows my lead enough that his breathing evens, his eyes become a bit more focused, and he notices me.

"Crazy, I'm so fucking sorry."

My chin trembles at the sound of his broken voice. "I know." With so many things unknown, he could be apologising for anything, so I take it. I hold it in my heart and hope this is just goodbye for now. "But we don't have to do this now, okay?"

"I just—" Too exhausted to talk, he rises, our eyes locked only one another. "I'm sorry I just need some fucking air, okay? Just a minute to think."

Nodding in understanding, I step away from him and watch him walk away from the both of us.

Turning to Sasha, I expect to see victory, but all I see is contempt and anger. On a mission, I stand in front of her. Toe to toe. Thinking about the man she supposedly loves, the man who is literally crippled by the pain she causes.

Uncomfortable I'm in her space, she steps back, making sure there's distance between us. I push my own hurt from earlier aside, and with the thought of her having the power to ruin my happiness, I let the venom spew.

"You know, I want to tell you how fucking selfish you are." She jerks her head back at my tone, but I just keep at it. "How your schemes are like poison, picking the perfect time to ruin *everything*."

"That man." I point to the direction Drix left in. "That remarkable, selfless, magnificent fucking man has been at your mercy for too long. He is the perfect friend, the perfect uncle, and the perfect brother, and you insist on reducing him to nothing."

The adrenaline pumping in my veins fuels my loose lips. "I will never know how he loved someone so fucking manipulative for so long."

I have to give it to her, she doesn't shrivel under my heated stare, or any accusation, she just takes it, probably knowing it's the truth.

"If you love him, choose him, Sasha. Don't throw chaos at him just because you can't stand the thought of anybody else having him. Be fucking sure because he is pure gold, and you treat him like nothing but trash."

"That—" she interrupts and I shake my head and hand.

"Just set him free. Let the world experience the full potential of this beautiful man, when he isn't chained to you and your indecisiveness."

She cocks her hip and crosses her hands over her chest. "You mean send him running into your arms."

"Any woman would be lucky to have him. I noticed that," I say pointing to my chest. "You didn't."

I school my features, trying to reason with her. "Just. Let. Him. Go."

"What if he doesn't choose either of us?"

Her question proves to me, she's as one track minded as I thought, because this isn't about who he chooses, this is about sacrificing your own needs for the person you love. But there's no point explaining that to someone like her. Instead, I bite back with the bitchiness she deserves. "I'll still fucking die happy, knowing it wasn't you."

"You're a bitch," she huffs.

"Maybe that's why he likes us both."

Placing Dakota's tickets on the table, I take the silent living room as the perfect time for my escape. Leaving Sasha in the room, I choose not to find Drix. With the high from my confrontation with Sasha dwindling, I feel the cracks in my chest return. And I need to get out of here before I bleed out.

Just as I'm about to pull the front door open, I hear a familiar voice. "Taylah," Em whisper-shouts. "Where are you going?"

I twist to see her, my hand still on the handle. "Why are you whispering?"

"I don't know," she says, continuing to whisper. "That's what people do in tense situations."

I give half a laugh. "Tense, huh?"

"Are you okay?" She grabs my wrist and pulls it off the cool metal.

"I don't know. I think I'm having an out of body experience and I need to get home before it all hits at once and I unravel in public."

"Drix is outside."

I shrug at her statement because I really have no idea what his side is to any of this, and after he left me stranded for most of the day, I'm pretty sure I know where his head's at right now.

"Let me drive you," she insists.

"I just want to be alone, Em." I lean forward and give her a quick kiss on the cheek. "I'll talk to you soon."

"Will you answer my calls?"

"Probably not." She rolls her eyes, and I open the front door. "Oh," I say, looking back. "You might want to check on Sasha in the room. Don't let her miss the rest of Dakota's party."

She salutes me, and I wave bye.

I need to get out of here.

I walk into my room, and my sad face stares back at me. The reminder that I will get through this screaming at me, like I drew her for this very moment. Tugging at my clothes, I pull them off and kick them to the side of the room.

I find one of Drix's t-shirts, smelling exactly like him, and wear it. I bunch up the material and bring it to my nose, the smell of wood and soap comforts and kills me all in one breath. I grab my phone and let Phil Collins' voice lull me into a false sense of hope, while I crawl into bed and nurse my wounds.

Putting angry thoughts of Sasha out of my mind, I let myself cry, acknowledging just how much I'm going to miss him. I think of any single moment that could've changed this outcome between us, or something I could've done to have avoided this feeling. But there's nothing.

I should've known it was always going to end up like this. His heart was divided, and I chose to ignore it. Drunk on love, I believed something so new, and short, could outlast whatever connection he has to his past.

As the tears continue, I cry for the unknown, I cry for what we had, I cry even more for how much heartache he's endured, and I cry over the end of the best thing to ever happen to me.

Eventually, he and I will have to say goodbye properly, and I'll tell him, it wasn't the little things that hurt the most, it was the loss of all the big things he and I can't have.

The house. The kids. The future.

If he was in front of me right now, I would give him one last kiss goodbye and say thank you for the memories. I will remember him with a smile, and gratitude because there's nothing negative to take away, except we weren't meant to be.

There's nothing to fault Hendrix Michaels for, except having a heart big enough to fit two women inside.

twenty four

HENDRIX

TWO WEEKS LATER

All I've done is sleep and eat and go to work. Every day is on repeat and every thought is on rotation.

Any time I've ever imagined Sasha saying those words to me, I felt pure elation. Like nothing in the world would ever top having her in my life, as mine, after all this time.

But then Taylah happened, and even the reality of Sasha wanting to be mine isn't enough to subside the ache in my chest.

I miss her. More than I ever thought I could. I miss her despite the mess my head is in, and I miss her despite the last fifteen years of my life feeling like one big lie.

I want to run into her arms, and beg her to never let me go. I let myself love her, through all the bullshit she pushed through, and I won't ever be able to forget her.

I love her.

I just don't know what to do from here on out. I don't know how to move past the pain and bring myself back to her.

I expected the fight with Sasha at the party. She does that, she's always done that with me. Pushed and pulled any chance she got. But when she told me she was ready, and she kissed me. My heart broke because the woman I loved for so long, didn't know me at all.

She was hoping I would kiss her back. Relapse. Forget about the woman that chose to put me back together, because she spent so much time pulling me apart.

My biggest heartache is seeing Sasha in a different light. It's painful, and it's life changing. The fact that I should've seen it so much sooner, has me hating myself more than I ever thought I could.

I hate myself for loving her for so long. I hate myself for giving her the power over my life that she didn't deserve. And I hate her, because now I feel weak and undeserving.

I think I loved the idea of Sasha and I, more than I actually loved her. I wanted what was supposed to rightfully be mine, and I wanted to show the world that perseverance pays off. I was in love with the sweet and innocent girl who told me I light up her world, except I couldn't see that we were both growing and changing. We were no longer those people, no matter how bad I wanted it to be true.

If I met Sasha today, had no history with her, and wasn't the uncle to her daughter, she wouldn't be the woman for me.

But if I met Taylah today and didn't have all those things to contend with, I'd already be on one knee telling her she's the one.

In all this, Taylah is the prize, I just have to show her I'm worthy enough to win.

Lost in a mountain of paperwork that needed to be brought home, I mishear the soft knocks at my front door. Getting louder, the noise registers, and I head to open up. Expecting Jagger, who has threatened numerous times to show up and pull me out of my funk, I'm surprised to see Sasha on the other side of my door.

Wearing baggy clothes, sporting dark circles under her eyes, and biting her nails. I haven't seen her look this out of sorts since Dakota was born.

"What's wrong? Is Dakota okay?"

"Of course she is," she says looking confused. "Why would you think that?"

"Because I can't think of any other reason you would feel the need to show up here."

The hostility in my voice doesn't even take time to warm up, Sasha's presence sending it into overdrive quicker than I expected.

"Drix, don't be like that."

"Please, don't tell me how to be. Don't you think you've done enough of that?"

Looking moderately embarrassed, she averts her eyes before asking if we can take it inside. Swinging the door open with enough force for her to get the hint. She walks in and makes herself comfortable on my couch.

"What is so important, you needed to come over?"

"You don't think you've avoided me enough? It's been two weeks. I've been waiting to hear from you."

"To hear about what?"

"Us. Together."

The words *us* and *together* does nothing. My heart doesn't jumpstart, my mind doesn't race into the future, and I can't even muster a smile. "You can't be serious, Sasha?"

Her eyes widen incredulously. "What's wrong with you? Of course I'm serious."

"Sash." I sit beside her on the couch, ridding myself of the tension, choosing my words carefully. "I don't want to be with you. I don't love you."

Her tears fall, and it's the time I would usually stop. I would do my best to rid her of the pain and coddle her as best I could, but those days are over. "And while you think it stings, you'll realise you don't love me either."

She doesn't protest, and it alleviates the small amount of guilt I have.

"You love the idea of me. The idea of us, and if we get together now, it's just going to be another six months or a year of our lives, where we could be with people that make us so much happier."

"Like Taylah."

At the mention of her name, every broken piece inside me begins to meld itself together. Sasha talking about Taylah should sting. There should be internal conflict and worry that whichever I choose, the grass may be greener on the other side. But it doesn't happen. The conflict doesn't come. And I know without a shadow of a doubt. I'm going to make her mine.

"Exactly, like Taylah."

"You really love her, don't you?"

I wipe away her tears and kiss the top of her head. "I really fucking love her."

I move off the couch and walk to my front door. It's a little rude and abrasive, but this isn't just figurative, I need to literally shut the door on this part of my life, to finally be able to chase the next part.

"When it's time, I'll tell her and hopefully I'll be worthy enough of her."

She catches on to my movements and meets me at the door. She looks at me with sad eyes, and I look at her with a clear mind.

"You're more than worthy, Drix." She kisses me on the cheek before heading out the door. "Don't ever let someone make you feel otherwise."

twenty five

SASHA

Running my fingers through Dakota's hair she falls asleep while watching *Home and Away.* Sneakily, I drag her phone out of her grasp and hope she has a number I need.

Just as I thought, it's there. Sending it to myself, I grab my phone off the armrest and do the most noble thing I have ever done in my life.

Me: *Love him right. Love him better.*

twenty six

TAYLAH

Emerson clicks her tongue in disapproval. "Seriously, that's not what you're wearing out to my birthday."

I look down at the casual black ensemble I paired with heels to "perk it up," and shrug, "It works for me."

"It's not your birthday," she sasses. "You don't get the last say."

"My outfit isn't your gift."

"Make it my gift. Go and change."

"For fuck's sake," I shout into the air. "Who even put you in charge?"

"Stop your whining, we have a reservation and I don't want to be late."

"Late for who? It's your birthday."

She waves me off. "I put some clothes on your bed. You've got twenty minutes. Make it happen."

"Fucking diva," I mutter.

There on my bed is my black dress. The black dress that started it all. It's been five weeks and I feel like my whole heart has been ripped out of my chest. I think about him constantly, and I miss him so much it borderline's unhealthy.

He filters through every thought in my mind, and every space in my house. His memory is paralysing, and I just don't know how to get past it.

Emerson mentioned he hasn't seen or spoken to anyone since it happened, but I shut down the conversation as quickly as I could. I didn't need a reason to wonder why he hasn't come to me. To tell me we're over, or to tell me we're not.

Some days when I'm feeling extra masochistic, I let myself revel in his silence and give myself false hope, that he's coming back. He just needs time.

Emerson bangs on the door. "I don't hear you getting ready, you've got ten minutes."

What a fucking ball buster.

Grabbing the dress, I put it on through tears, and get ready for him. I tell myself the lie, because I really don't know what to do if he's not the be all and end all for me.

For the first time ever I can sympathise with my mother telling me she wanted to grieve for the love of her life on her own.

Drix isn't dead, but I feel like I'm grieving all the same. And every time I think I can rejoin the world and put it all behind me, my heart tells me it's not time yet.

My bedroom door swings open, and Emerson barges in. Prepared to reprimand me for breathing incorrectly, the expression on her face is mildly surprised that I'm actually dressed and ready to go.

"See? Look how pretty you are. Don't you feel better?"

I give her my best clenched teeth smile. "Couldn't be better," I grit out.

"Chop. Chop. Young lady," she says while clapping at me. "Let's go."

Deciding to completely ignore her for the rest of the night. I lock up the house and jump in her car. It takes us forty-five minutes to arrive to what I thought was a restaurant and is now a karaoke bar.

"Karaoke?" My voice cracks in surprise.

She narrows her eyes at me. "Is there a problem?"

"Since when do you sing?"

"Sometimes I like to try different things."

"Biggest crock of shit I ever heard," I mutter underneath my breath. She's the worst liar.

"God, you are in the shittiest mood," she snaps. "Could you please get over it."

"Fine. I'm sorry." I give her a quick peck on the cheek. "You're right. It's your birthday, and I will have fun with you tonight." I offer her my pinky. "I promise."

Stepping into the karaoke bar, I'm surprised to see it's set up similar to a restaurant. It's got all different sized tables that face the stage, and a bar to order food and drinks from. Expecting to see more of Emerson's other friends, I'm surprised when she sits us at a table of two.

"Where's everyone else?" I ask.

"It's just you and me."

"I wouldn't have minded if other people came," I say feeling guilty. "I know I've been a dick to be around, but I would've played nice for your birthday."

She puts her hand over mine, while softly shaking her head. "It's not that. I just wanted it to be you and me."

"Fair enough." I look around and take in people are only sitting and there's piano music in the background. "Where's the singing?"

"It starts when they begin serving dinner."

"Oh. When can we order?"

"Friday nights are set menus only," she says quickly, hoping I won't pull her up on it.

"Emmmmmmm," I groan.

"Shut up. It's only you and me, and you can eat extra if you need to."

Surprised by how busy this hole in the wall is, I'm looking forward to everyone singing badly in public.

The waitress appears out of thin air with our entrees and the portions have me a little less miffed that I have to share with Em.

The lights dim a little bit further, when this cute pixie looking lady, bursts out onto the stage, ready to officiate the night. Her energy is contagious, and I find myself feeling a little giddy at what's to come.

"Okay, ladies and gentlemen, before we get into the messy, drunk, and off-key part of the evening. I have someone who has put in a special request, for a very special person."

The crowd cheers and my stomach unexpectedly erupts into flutters. I look over at Em, and her face says it all. She leans over the table. Kissing me on the cheek and whispering in my ear. "Be happy. Love you."

My eyes stay fixated ahead as the spotlight shines on the centre of the stage, and out comes my one and my only; Hendrix Michaels. Brown mussed up hair, a navy blue t-shirt, paired with dirty, dark denim jeans and Chucks, he looks as perfect as I remember. He looks out into the crowd, seeking me out. When he finds me, he tips his head to the lady, giving her the go ahead.

The familiar music starts, and I have to bury my head in my hands to control my emotions. He jumps off the stage, gunning for me, as Phil Collins' "Groovy Kind of Love" plays throughout the whole place. It's everything. Tragically cheesy, and so fucking perfect.

The wait for him to reach me becomes too much. I kick off my heels, hike my dress up, and run. Tears streaming down my face with every step. Getting closer, he holds out his arms and I throw myself into the only place I belong.

Securing me tightly, I cry the happiest tears of my life, all over his shoulder. The song ends, when I feel his hand shoot up and circle in the air.

Setting me on my feet, I see the relief and unshed tears in his eyes, as the song starts up again. Cradling my neck, he brings me to him, close enough that even air would struggle to get in between.

I feel his hot breath spread like wildfire all over my body as he says my favourite line. "Sing for me, Crazy."

twenty seven

TAYLAH

I wake up still floating on cloud nine. I look over at Hendrix, who looks so good in my bed, I could cry. Again.

Reaching for my phone, I pull up the message I got from an unknown number and write back.

Me: *I will*

epilogue

HENDRIX

TWO YEARS LATER

Picking up the keys from the real estate agent, I rush home to give Taylah and the girls their final surprise.

After months of searching we finally found our dream home; one big enough for Aubrey, Abigail, and everyone else who comes in and out of our lives.

It's been two years since I walked back into Taylah's life, and I have no regrets. Actually, I have one, that we didn't meet sooner so I would have more years with her, because this lifetime and the next will never be enough.

From then on, our relationship hit the ground running and we still haven't stopped. It took three months for me to sell my place and move in with her. She argued we should move into my place because it was bigger, but I told her I wasn't ready to give up her drawing to strangers.

One year later, we put down our names as foster parents. It's been challenging, rewarding, and completely life-changing, in all the ways that matter.

It's an open house for the most part. Long term and short term stays until we met Aubrey and Abigail. They were newborn twins who needed permanent housing. It was kismet.

Seeing Taylah work her magic, and bring her *Crazy t*o more lives than just mine has been the icing on the cake. So much so, that I can't wait to have babies of our own.

Walking in the front door, I greet her the same way I always do. "Honey, I'm home."

Lying on the couch, she has two babies draped across her body; the three of them sleeping. I snap a picture, and send it to her, with the hashtag MILF. Instagram is still a no go for me, but nobody can say I don't have my hashtags down pat.

Using the time they're asleep to pack some last minute things in the car, I walk around the house making as much noise as possible. She's going to kill me, but I'm desperate for them to wake up.

Two hours later, we pull up to the place dreams are made of.

"I'm just going to check something inside, are you good to get the girls out of the car?" She rolls her eyes at me while shutting the door with her hip.

"I don't know, Sexy, it's a mystery how the three of us survive without you."

I kiss her to shut her smart mouth up. It works, and she knows it. "I'll see you inside."

The sound of slow and cautious footsteps sets my plan in motion. The front door opens straight to the living room, a huge blank wall with no furniture directly in front of it. Down on one bended knee, I hold both her ring and a photo I've kept hidden in one hand.

Her mouth drops the minute she sees me. Placing the girls in the middle of the floor, she frets about their comfort before walking toward me. *This is why I love her.*

"What are you doing?" she asks as she gets closer.

"What do you think I'm doing, Crazy?" I fight the urge to stand up and continue with the plan. "I want you to marry me."

"Drix." She says my name like the sun rises and sets with me. Like there's nothing before me and nothing after me. She says my name like I'm the one.

Every. Single. Time.

"Crazy, when you walked into my world, I knew you would change it. I didn't know how or in what way, but you were someone I was never going to forget. You had faith in me when I lost hope for my own happy ever after. You challenge me to be better, to do better. For you, for our family, and for myself."

Holding my hand out for hers, I slide the ring on her fourth finger, just as I hand her the next surprise.

"What's this?" she asks.

"See if you remember it," I urge.

Her eyes widen, as it dawns on her. "How did you get this?"

"I had it taken that night." In her hand is a photo from the karaoke bar. Smiling through tears, this photo doesn't hold the same sadness as the original. It's the change that I take all the credit for. The moment might capture her happiness instead of her pain, but it shows off her ethereal beauty all the same. "Turn it around."

NEXT CHAPTER

"Taylah Jennings, I love you. I have never loved someone as much as I love you. I have never been loved the way you love me. Become my wife. Become the mother of our children, all of them, in any which way they come. Save the world with me, Crazy. Just like you saved me."

Head to my website for a bonus scene.

www.marleyvbooks.com

Enjoy **REVIVE**?

Have you read the next book in the Redemption Series?

Read on for the synopsis of Sasha's story.

rectify

marley valentine

We weren't just young, we were stupid and reckless.

He was the beginning of every bad decision I made,
the enemy of everyone I'd ever loved.

I was a pawn in his game. A prize to be claimed,
and a trophy to be flaunted.

Now we're two adults with crooked pasts,
trying to straighten out our future.

His heart belongs to his daughter,
while mine is too tattered to give away.

Neither of us believe in happily ever after.

Not after everything we've been through.

So, why are we desperately trying to chase ours?

acknowledgements

Thank you. Yes, you. For purchasing, borrowing, reading and reviewing. I couldn't do any of it without you.

Andrew and Jax, you're my world. I love you.

Steph. There's nothing better than sharing books with someone. There's nothing better than sharing books with your best friend.

Mum, thank you for reading these.

Jacob and Laura. Man, how do you guys even put up with all this craziness? Thank you for pushing me over the line, each and every time.

Diane, you are the best decision I ever made.

Aubrey, you keep getting better and better. Bring on 2018.

Marley's MOFO's I hope this book was everything you wanted it to be. Let's all be #TeamDrix.

Celia Aaron, Autumn Grey, Kacey Shea, Bianca Smith, Brenda Travers, Donna Elsegood and Ella Fields. You woman are my constants. Always willing to listen. Always willing to help.

A HUGE thank you to Alexis Alvarez who took the time to read Revive and offer so much of her time and advice to make it better.

Michelle and Shauna, you ladies kept this book alive, and I love you for it.

Ellie McLove, I LOVE YOU.

Laura from Hawkeyes Proofing, the best thing about you is I can send you anything at anytime and you read it. With so many of your own deadlines you made this book a priority. Thank you.

Enticing Journey, I love working with you. Not sure if you would say the same thing about me though LOL.

If I forgot someone. I'm sorry. I still love you, and you know the drill… Eat McDonalds on the regular and stalk Charlie Hunnam

Much Peace and Love.

about marley valentine

Marley Valentine comes from the future. Living in Sydney, Australia with her family, when she's not busy writing her own stories, she spends most of her time immersed in the words of her favourite authors.

Marley Valentine is also half of Remy Blake; a male and female author duo, paired up to have some fun writing steamy, short reads with insta love/lust and a HEA. You can expect twice the debauchery in every novel they write.

For more on Marley visit her website:

www.marleyvbooks.com

Made in the USA
Columbia, SC
14 August 2023